RESCUING KENNA

GHOST LEGACY
BOOK 3

PJ FIALA

RT
ROLLING
THUNDER

DEDICATION

I've had so many wonderful people come into my life and I want you all to know how much I appreciate it. From each and every reader who takes the time out of their days to read my stories and leave reviews, thank you.

My beautiful, smart and fun Road Queens, who play games with me, post fun memes, keep the conversation rolling and help me create these captivating characters, places, businesses and more. Thank you ladies for your ideas, support and love. The following characters and places were created by:

Nicky Ortiz - **GHOST Headquarters** - The HOG (Home, Office and Garage)

House name ideas

Amy Ball - The Stitchery

Deb Jones Diem - Hemmed In

Kerry Harteker - Mending Box

Karen Cranford LeBeau - Button Down

Julia Murphy - Zipped Tight

Gail Whitley - Needle Point

Dana Zamora - Sown Home

People:
Alana Ackerman - Ryhs
Liz Bradley - Officer Maria Bradley
Tjuana TJ Brown - Shianne Brown
Lyne Carroll & Belinda Jackson Hercule -Elena Dorsey
Cathy Christmas – Helissa, GHOST Cook
Terri DeMario - Flynn DeMario
Anna Marie Flamini - Amelia (childhood friend of Elena)
Peggy Fowler and Sharon R. Cowan - Kenna Lawrence
Kerry Harteker - Elena's mom's health issues
Belinda Jackson Hercule - Sharon Jackson
Ginna Honeycutt - Officer Carter Gordon
Beckie Johnson Lowe - Colt Lowe
Nathalie Juergensen - Daniel Juergensen
Killaine Kennedy - Niya Lawrence
Kristi Hombs Kopydlowski - Lara Bennit and Troy Brown
Kim Kurtz - Howie Lawrence
Karen Cranford LeBeau - Klaire Brown, Aidyn Dunbar,
Sheriff Rex Cranford and Millie LeBeau
Elinda Moody - Keaton Bennit
Monique Mousseau - Spencer Lawson
Julia Murphy - Atty. Peter Murphy, Alan
Terra Oenning - Rayleigh Winters
Nicky Ortiz - Explosives Expert from Brookswood - Dylan
Cindy Pearson - Ami Pearson
Pamela Reveal - Matthew Vickers
Jayne Smith - Atty. Francesca Smith
Yolanda Tobiasen - Laylah Bennit
Elizabeth Ward Sadowsky - Chesson Ward
Jo West - Baxter Fenshaw
Dana Zamora - Sean and Jonathon Lawrence
Jessica Zoe - Grace Dorsey

Places:
Amy Barber - Fort Abraham
Kim Kurtz - Glen Hollow
Kathy Franklin - Hickory Hills
Monique Mousseau Westwood - Brookswood

Glen Hollow businesses -
Abigail Capps - Paxton's General Store
Abigail Capps - Squeaky Clean Laundromat
Nancy Hoch - Homemade in the Hollow, Stackable Reads
Bookstore
Nathalie Juergensen - Barbershop - Hairy Beards and The
Broken Barrel
Beckie Johnson Lowe - Chestnut Grove
Nicky Ortiz - Divine Designs, Lady Liberty Law Office,
The Paper Trail and Porter's Steakhouse
Anne Walker - Lara's Delights
Jo West - Bloomin' Lovely
PJF - Smith Squared Attorneys at Law

Black Road Resistance (BRR)
Jamie Rogers - BRR Black Road Resistance
Ronda Barnes-Howard - Everett Howard
Jayne Smith - Craig Howard
Marlene Davis - Hanalore Howard
Sally Harris - Brock Harris
Ginna Honeycutt - Cole Honeycutt
Lynne Kerr - Gerard Weston
Karen Cranford LeBeau - Brenner Matthews, Ramsey
Stewart
Beckie Johnson Lowe - Brayden Lowe
Lisa Mansfield - Reece Mansfield
Mary Lou Melzer - Kent Bennit

Arlene Miklovic - Liliana Weston
Julie Ann Price - Liam Price
Jayne Smith - Theresa
Jo West - Jasiah Weston
Debbie Zsidai - Medicine Woman - Elenor

Last but not least, my family for the love and sacrifices
they have made and continue to make to help me achieve
this dream, especially my husband and best friend, Gene.
Words can never express how much you mean to me.
To our veterans and current serving members of our
armed forces, police and fire departments, thank you
ladies and gentlemen for your hard work and sacrifices;
it's with gratitude and thankfulness that I mention you in
this forward.

Enjoy this steamy small-town protector romance by USA Today bestselling author PJ Fiala.

He's a GHOST operative trying to keep the peace.

She's a process server determined to do her job.

Together they are caught up in a war neither will back down from.

When the job can only be handled by the team that doesn't exist, you call GHOST.

Spencer Lawson has observed the criminal behavior of the people of Hickory Hills Kentucky and knows they are dangerous. When the police chief walks into the GHOST compound with a battered and bruised Kenna Lawrence, Spencer's protective hackles raise. As he watches Kenna's determination to do her job, he knows she's in danger, but she won't heed his warnings.

When unsuspecting Kenna comes to town and finds herself in a predicament of having to serve court documents to the leader of Hickory Hills, she finds out quickly they won't have anything to do with the US government. Not only that, they give her a small taste of what will happen if she comes up their mountain again.

When Kenna is caught in a war between right and wrong, Spencer will do everything in his power to *Rescue Kenna.*

Rescuing Kenna is the third novel in the GHOST Legacy Romantic Suspense Series, although all books in the GHOST Legacy world can be read as stand alones. A steamy romantic story with a guaranteed happily ever after, it does have some strong language and exciting sexy times. Enjoy Spencer and Kenna!

GLOSSARY - GHOST LEGACY

The next gen GHOST are all grown up and living on missions of their own. Meet these men and women of GHOST Legacy.

Tate Vickers - Tate is the son of Gaige and Sophie Vickers. Their story is told in Defending Sophie. Tate is a recon specialist and runs the GHOST satellite office.

Aidyn Dunbar - Is the son of Bridget and Axel Dunbar. You can find their story is Defending Bridget. Aidyn's specialty is hand-to-hand combat.

Spencer Lawson - Spencer is the son of Wyatt and Yvette Lawson. You can read their story in Defending Yvette. Spencer specialize's in security, recon and recovery.

Henry Delany - Henry is the son of Hawk and Roxanne Delany. Their story is told is Defending Roxanne. His specialties are recon, recovery, and anything that requires size.

Adelaide Masters - Adelaide's parents are Josh and Isabella Masters. Their story is told in Defending Isabella. Adelaide served in the Army and is the team's medic.

Maya Sager - Maya served in the US Marine Corps.

Her parents are Dodge and Jax Sager. Their story is told in Finding His Jewel. Maya's specialty is recon and rescue.

Myles Sager - Myles served in the US Marine Corps. Myles and Maya are the twins of Dodge and Jax Sager. Myles is an explosives expert.

1

Spencer ducked under a tree branch and continued running. He had to catch the shithead who just cut his wires at the construction site and take him in. The BRR had been quiet for the past couple of months. Now this. It always seemed as though they took two steps forward and one back. And it rankled that they always focused on his wiring. He'd rewired this entire construction site on at least two occasions over the past year.

He jumped over a low [illegible], then bent to dip under a lean-to roof in the back of the laundromat.

The dark head turned a corner, and his heels beat the ground. He rounded the corner and saw the kid or man, or whoever, duck between Divine Designs and The Broken Barrel, the local bar, which furrowed his brows. Why the kid didn't run up the mountain confused him.

Spencer darted across the road. A passing car laid on his horn as he went by. Absently waving, he kicked up his pace. Nowhere. The dark-haired boy was nowhere to be seen.

Stopping to catch his breath, hands on his knees, he focused on his breathing and heart rate.

"Shit."

He stood and looked in every direction but saw no signs of the kid he'd been chasing. Shaking his head, he turned toward the construction site.

His phone rang. "Yeah."

"Did you catch him?" Henry asked.

"No. He just disappeared."

"People don't just disappear."

"Right."

Henry chuckled, and it was the equivalent of nails on a chalkboard right about now. It was better not to respond.

"You need a ride?"

"No. I'm on my way back now. I'll be there shortly."

Henry's chuckling cut off, and he dropped his phone into his pocket. He rotated his head and stretched his shoulders.

His phone rang again and this time his irritation shot up tenfold.

"What?"

"Well, Spencer Lawson, this is Sheriff Cranford. I'd like to have a word with you and Henry if you have a few minutes. Tate said I should speak to you two. I can be out at the construction site in about fifteen minutes, if that works."

He huffed out a breath and closed his eyes. He stopped walking for a moment, then replied. "I'm sorry, Sheriff. I thought you were Henry calling to razz me."

Sheriff Cranford chuckled. "I'm sorry to disappoint."

"No disappointment. I'm on my way back to the construction site right now. I should be back by the time you get there."

"Alright, I'll see you in a few minutes."

The line went dead and he pocketed his phone once again. He jogged toward the base. This time the pace was steady and on paved surfaces instead of the little jaunt that kid just took him on through the woods before leading into town.

A truck drove by with a fishing boat hooked onto the back and another truck followed that one with UTVs on a trailer. Someone was going to have fun. He cut between the flower shop and the laundromat, waving to the ladies outside Bloomin' Lovely as he jogged down First Street to connect to the county road that would take him to the construction site.

A moving truck pulled into the corner parking lot. There was a business there called The Paper Trail. He'd never checked out just what it was. Maya thought it was about scrapbook stuff. Glancing at his watch, he determined he had ten minutes before the sheriff would be at the site. Spencer stepped up his pace—and crashed.

He caught her but lost his footing and fell with her. Spencer rolled, absorbing the brunt of the fall with his right shoulder.

"Oof."

He rolled to his back, holding onto a woman, which meant she now laid on top of him. Mail sailed through the air. A white envelope landed on his head before sliding off. Other envelopes lay around them.

When his eyes finally focused, he saw the prettiest pair of green eyes he'd ever seen. Her lashes were long and full. Almond-shaped eyes. She had a cute little beauty mark on the top of her left cheek, near the outer corner of her eye.

She licked her lips, and the shine caught his attention.

"Are you alright?"

Her voice was breathy.

"Yeah. You?" He smiled. "I mean, are you alright?"

She still laid on top of his body and he realized his arms were still wrapped around her.

"Yeah."

She moved to slide off to the right side and his body responded to her movements.

She scrambled to her feet and dusted her burgundy slacks and matching blazer with her hands. He stared for a minute, then stood and assessed his shoulder. Rotating it slightly, he felt it twinge, but it would be fine.

Her eyes moved to his shoulder. She touched his shirt. "You've ripped your shirt."

"It'll be fine. Helissa will take care of it."

She nodded. "That's good."

She stooped and began picking up the mail she'd been carrying. He helped her, then suddenly realized he owed her an apology.

"I'm so sorry. I didn't see you."

She swept her long, dark hair over her shoulders and shrugged. "It may have been my fault. I was looking over the mail as I walked to the box here," she gestured...left, "and I wasn't paying attention."

She smiled, and he could have stared at her for days.

She shrugged. "If you're alright, I really need to get going. I have a meeting."

Taking a step back, he held his hands up. "No worries. I'm fine. I have to get going, too."

She nodded, put the envelopes into the mailbox, lifted the red flag and turned to the building behind her. The Paper Trail.

He waited until she disappeared through the door and

turned toward the site once again, this time he'd be more careful.

As he jogged onto the construction site, the sheriff's squad car was in the lot. "Shit." He jogged to the office and didn't hesitate to enter.

The sheriff sat in a chair, speaking with Baxter Fenshaw, the general contractor, and Henry Delany, one of his teammates.

The sheriff turned. "Well, there he is." The sheriff's eyes landed on his shoulder and the ripped shirt then slid up to his face.

"Are you alright?"

"Yeah. Took a tumble."

Henry raised his eyebrows in question. Spencer shook his head, grabbed a water and took a seat.

Henry cleared his throat. "The sheriff wanted to chat with us about some help to serve papers on Craig Howard."

"Okay. Why wouldn't a process server do that?"

The sheriff leaned forward. "Well, the BRR are being sued. Specifically, Craig. For property damages and medical bills suffered by Flynn DeMario from the gas station. I don't think he's going to take it well. We only have one process server in town and he's in his sixties."

Spencer felt his eyebrows shoot into his hairline when the construction door opened.

She walked into the office. Confident. Gorgeous. And the scuff across the side of her shiny burgundy high heels barely marred her impeccable attire.

2

She stared at the group of men sitting in the construction office. Which looked like organized chaos. Maps of varying shapes and sizes littered the walls, stuck up by mismatched thumbtacks and straight pins. The little table that held the coffeepot had spilled sugar and coffee grounds on it, and the eight-foot table next to it had more maps and rolled up papers laying on it.

"Well, Kenna Lawrence, is that you?"

She glanced at Sheriff Rex Cranford. She hadn't seen him in years.

"Yes, Sheriff Cranford, it's me."

Sheriff Cranford sat forward in his chair and looked at the two men sitting next to him. "Kenna Lawrence, this here is Henry Delany and Spencer Lawson. Over here is Baxter Fenshaw, the construction manager."

Spencer stood and held his hand out to her. "It's nice to meet you." He had a sly grin on his handsome face but said nothing of their earlier run-in.

"It's nice to meet you too."

Henry, the other man, was big, as big as she'd ever

seen not on a football field. He stretched his hand out. "Ma'am. Nice to meet you."

She shook his hand and nodded, and he sat. Spencer still stood. She noticed he moved to the left of his chair and held his hand out to it. "Please take a seat."

She sat, feeling incredibly out of place. Sheriff Cranford started the conversation. "Kenna, when did you get back to town and where's your daddy?"

Where's your daddy? Damn it, she hated this. Just because she's a woman, others looked at her as if she was too delicate to do her job.

"I got back to town a couple days ago, and my daddy is at home. He's been having issues with his heart and the doctor has him on bedrest until all his tests come back. He asked me to come back home and help him for a while. So, as soon as he's better, I'm going back to Houston."

"I didn't hear a darned thing about his heart. I'm sorry to hear that."

She shrugged. "It was sudden. He's been having episodes, but he's hidden them from everyone. It does no good to let others know how frail you are when you're trying to serve papers on them."

"Well, that's true enough."

The sheriff looked up at Spencer and nodded. "Spencer and Henry here can deliver your papers to Craig Howard. I understand that Flynn DeMario is suing Craig for damages and personal injury. With the recent events, I don't think it's safe for you to go up there alone."

"No." She blurted it out, then took a deep breath and reminded herself to stay off the defensive. "I can handle it. I've been serving papers since I was eighteen years old. It's our family business."

Sheriff Cranford leaned forward. "I know you've been

doing this a long time, Kenna. And the family business and all. But I don't think you understand what you're up against here." Sheriff Cranford looked at Spencer. "Tell her Spencer."

He cleared his throat, and she watched his Adam's apple bob as he swallowed. That led her eyes to his broad shoulders and the tear in his shirt. Then she remembered his powerful arms wrapped around her waist and her cheeks felt warm.

"Recently, Craig has been incredibly unpredictable. Gerard Weston and his son, Jasiah, have been trying to manage him, from what little we're told, but he's not happy about the changes up there and he sure will not be happy having papers served on him."

"I understand that. Believe it or not, nearly every person I serve is mad about it. So that's nothing new for me."

Henry glanced her way. "But Craig is unpredictable in a way that is deadly. When Elena left with Aidyn, their very livelihood left with them. They don't have a brewer and they don't have a way to make money. Not the money they used to make from the elixir. Some of their people are coming down and selling their crafts and wooden furniture pieces. Some have gotten jobs. From what we've heard, Craig makes their lives hell up there because they're caving to the government's pressure."

She shook her head. "But I've served people just like him. Criminals, thieves, gun toting anti-establishment— you name it. I'm fine to do this on my own."

Henry turned to look at Spencer and she saw Spencer's jaw tighten. Sheriff Cranford leaned forward once again; the metal chair he sat in squeaked.

"Kenna. How about you let Spencer or Henry escort

you up the mountain? At least if anything were to happen, you'd have someone with some brawn to back you up."

Her shoulders dropped, and she realized she would get nowhere in here. She stood and nodded, first to the sheriff, then to Baxter, Henry, then she turned to Spencer. "I'll let you know how it goes once I've served him."

Her heels clipped across the floor, and she took steady breaths to keep from crying. She was so sick and tired of this "little woman" crap. It was the reason she left this town. Small towns tended to not change quickly. This one apparently hadn't changed at all. She'd been so hopeful.

Once she exited, she carefully navigated the metal steps so her heels didn't fall into a hole in the stairs and trip her. She watched her feet as she stepped down and noticed the scuff on her heel. "Dammit." She huffed. So much for her new shoes. She'd so hoped to come back to town and not be Howie Lawrence's little girl, but the woman she was.

Trouble was, she didn't have a job to go back to. When her parents called her to come back and help, she asked her boss for leave and he told her if she left, she was unemployed. In anger, she'd sent out resumés online as she packed to come home. As soon as she found another process service position, she'd go back to Houston and demand to be treated like a capable woman.

3

Spencer swore inwardly as she left. Stubborn. Clueless. Muleheaded, as his mom used to say about him. And she was going to get herself injured. Maybe killed. But what she didn't fully understand, was just how unpredictable Craig was right now.

"So, Spencer, what happened to you?"

He turned to the sheriff and realized they were all watching him watch Kenna Lawrence strut out the door. He shrugged his shoulders.

"I took a tumble while jogging. I looked down at my watch and wasn't paying attention."

The sheriff nodded but said nothing. His eyes shifted to Baxter's, and he grinned.

"Wouldn't have anything to do with the scuffs on her shoes, does it?"

He stared, not sure what to say. They'd done nothing wrong, and he told the truth, sort of. But he'd pretended not to know her when she walked in and that likely looked suspicious. Luckily, Baxter didn't give him anymore time before asking about the kid.

"So, what happened out there?"

Spencer shook his head. "Some kid cut my wires. I chased the little shit but couldn't catch him. Dark hair. About five foot six or seven. I've never seen him before."

Baxter slowly nodded. "How bad?"

Spencer dragged his hand through his hair. "I can get it fixed today."

"Sounds good."

He finished his bottle of water and tossed the empty bottle into the recycle bin before striding out of the trailer. He heard Henry stand and follow him, but he didn't look back. As his feet hit the dirt, he noticed the little divot on the ground from Kenna's heels and he rolled his shoulder again.

"Hey," Henry called.

"Yeah."

"Where did the kid go?"

He turned to Henry. "That kid ran into town. It's the weirdest thing. He kept going between the businesses, not up the hill."

Henry nodded and looked toward the mountain as they stood at the base. "I thought that was the direction he was heading. What do you make of that?"

"I don't know. Some of the BRR are coming down for jobs. So, does his dad or mom work down here and he was running toward them? Is he throwing me off?"

Henry looked down the road and sighed. "I don't know if we'll ever figure them out. What are the chances it's just some random kid from town pulling a stunt or dared to do it?"

"It seems pretty specific and the same thing the BRR has done repeatedly."

"That could be the dare."

Spencer shook his head. "I'm gonna reconnect those wires so we have cameras before we go home."

"Need help?"

"No. I've got it. You can finish your patrol around the perimeter if you want and I'll finish up the wiring, then we can go home."

He heard the crunching of tires on the gravel, so he crossed toward the tower where his damaged camera wiring waited. Turning, he froze when he saw Kenna Lawrence climbing out of her white Jeep.

She turned her head to him, and the sun glinted on her dark hair. She shrugged her shoulders. His feet ate up the distance between them, and he noticed she fidgeted slightly as he neared. Henry stopped across the grounds and watched.

"You're back."

Her smile didn't reach her eyes, and she bit the inside of her bottom lip before responding. "My dad said I needed someone to go up there with me the first time. Since his heart isn't healthy right now, I don't want to upset him and promised to come back for help."

Nodding, he grinned. "Okay. I'm happy to go up there with you."

"I'm sorry to bother you. But since you all thought it was best this way, I came back here rather than go to the sheriff."

"No worries." He turned toward Henry and pointed up the mountain. Henry nodded and continued walking around the perimeter. "Shall we go? We can take my truck."

"I don't mind driving up there."

He filled his lungs with air. "I know you don't mind, but how about we take my truck this time? They're used to seeing it up there and it might make things easier. Once you've been up there, you can take your own vehicle should you find the need to go on up again."

Her shoulders dropped slightly, but she nodded. "Okay. I'll just get my papers."

He stepped back as she opened the door to her Jeep and pulled out a folio that was about an inch thick. She slung a little black purse over her shoulder and turned to face him. "I'm ready."

Nodding, he held his hand out toward his truck, and they walked silently to it. He opened her door, which made her lips form a straight line, but she stepped on the running boards and hopped in without a word. After he closed the door, he shook his head, more to clear it than anything else, as he moved around his truck and climbed in.

He pulled from the parking area and turned them toward the black road that would take them up the mountain. "How much has your father told you about recent events here?"

"Not much. He's been sick, mostly. Lara told me about Kent, though."

"You know Lara?"

Kenna laughed. "I know practically everyone who's lived here for over five years."

Grinning, he nodded. "Makes sense." He turned them up the road. "What else did Lara tell you?"

Kenna watched the road as they traveled. Her eyes scanned the area around them as they ascended the hill. "Not much. Tate saved her from Kent's wrath. I heard about Lara's dad and mom. But she seems to be happy."

"Tate's a good man. I've known him most of my life.

Our parents all worked together. He's in love with Lara. It was apparent from the start."

"I'm glad. She's good and deserves someone who will treat her right."

The road turned and twisted, but he kept the pace steady. He slowed when they reached the area where they'd normally be stopped, but no one jumped out from the woods to stop them. "Hmm." He hadn't meant for her to hear, but she did.

"Hmm, what?"

He shrugged his shoulder. "Normally, someone would jump out right about here and stop us to ask questions, and we'd have to walk the rest of the way up. Which will not be easy in your heels."

"I have worn heels on terrain that would make you weak."

He laughed. "Okay. Someday I'll take you up on the challenge. I've been on some pretty tough terrain."

She grinned, but he said nothing further. He navigated another corner and there they were. Two men he'd never seen before, blocking the road with four-wheelers.

4

She was almost to the junk dump when she saw the two men. They wore dirty jeans and flannel shirts that looked too big for their bodies. Their expressions were less than friendly, and then Spencer exited the truck.

She kept her eyes on him as he moved toward the front of the truck, then paused. She couldn't hear what was being said, so she opened her door and stepped down. Immediately, she was sorry she'd done that when the two men drew closer.

Spencer introduced her. "This is Kenna Lawrence, and she has some papers for Craig."

"What kind of papers?" one man spat.

"The none-of-your-business kind." Spencer responded.

The man closest to Spencer took a step toward him, but to his credit, Spencer didn't move. He stood like a statue, and she had to admire his bravery.

"If you're going to be cocky—*Spencer* — we're going to have us some trouble."

"I'm not being cocky. Kenna has papers for Craig. How

do you think Craig would respond if he knew you were reading his private papers?"

"I wasn't going to read them. I just want to know."

Her heartbeat increased, and she moved a step closer. "I have court papers for Craig."

"He don't want no court papers."

"I understand." Her voice shook slightly, and she hated that. "I'm required by the court to make sure he gets them. I have to hand them to him myself."

Both men eyed her suspiciously, but she stood still like Spencer was doing and tried not to look scared.

"Hang on," the man in the blue shirt said. He got on his 4-wheeler and took off up the mountain road while the other stood staring at her.

Spencer diverted his attention by asking. "How are things going up there these days? I see a few of you have jobs down the mountain."

The glare he received in return was scary, but Spencer didn't seem to let it bother him.

"I'm not gonna sit here and chitchat with you."

Spencer shrugged and turned to her. "You want to chitchat?"

Her nerves got the better of her and she giggled. "Sure."

"So, as soon as we're finished delivering these papers to Craig, what are your plans?"

She swallowed because she thought he was going to ask her out on a date. And that conflicted her. Did she want to go on a date? Maybe. What could it hurt? He seemed nice enough. He was handsome and strong and brave, unlike some men she'd met lately.

"I'm... I've got some unpacking to do. Nothing super important."

Spencer nodded and grinned. "I'm going to eat, fire off some rounds in the range, then do nothing."

She felt her face fall. He wasn't asking her out. He was actually chitchatting.

"That sounds like a nice evening."

The motor of the 4-wheeler reached her ears and Spencer turned toward the sound. The second man jumped off his machine and crossed his arms over his chest.

"Craig said you can crawl down the mountain and die for all he cares. He doesn't want any of your court papers. Your court doesn't mean shit to him."

She was dumbfounded. "Regardless, it's my job to give him these papers."

"He doesn't care two shits about your job. Beat it."

Spencer turned to her, "Let's go Kenna."

"But I have to serve these papers. I can't just leave them. I have to hand them to him."

"Let's go. We'll talk about it on the way down."

"But..."

Spencer stepped right into her space. His voice lowered, and he whispered, "Let's go. We'll talk about it."

He touched her shoulder and gently turned her around. She followed him blindly without thinking. Mostly because her head was spinning. Spencer opened the passenger door, and she stepped into the truck and plopped on the seat. A big whoosh of air escaped her lungs as Spencer walked in front of the truck. He nodded at the two men watching them. One of them had a stupid grin on his stupid face. The other glared at her.

Spencer hopped in his truck and started it, then slowly backed them down the mountain road. At a turnout, he turned the truck around and moved them toward the bottom of the mountain.

"There are times, such as today, when Craig is not in the mood. There are other times he's curious to see what we have for him. Today, he wasn't in the frame of mind to talk to anyone. It's better for you to wait until he's more agreeable."

"How am I going to know when he's in the mood?"

"We'll come up and try again."

"How often?"

He glanced at her, and she swallowed. He was handsome. She'd met handsome men before, but there was something different about him.

"We can come back tomorrow and try again or wait a couple of days. Usually, it makes a difference who his gatekeepers are."

"Gatekeepers. As in, the two leering creeps up there?"

He nodded and his lips turned up on the right side. "Yeah. I think it's how they present the visitors to him. Those two were angry and hateful. So, my guess is he went into Craig with an attitude and Craig shut it down. Now, if someone else is watching the road, he can be more accommodating."

"Have you found him accommodating?"

"At times." Spencer dragged his long, masculine fingers through the waves of his hair, causing her to dwell on the contrast between soft and strong. "Sometimes his curiosity is aroused. I'm guessing, leading with the words 'court papers', set him off. Craig's angry right now about anything that has to do with our laws and the fact that some folks have come down the mountain to work. He's taking the money they're making to help pay off the taxes owed on the land up there. He's sort of caught between a rock and a hard place and it makes him a bit ragey."

"Ragey?" She giggled.

"His world is changing and he can't stop it. He can't control it. So, he's lashing out and controlling what he can. Today, that was a visitor who had court papers."

He turned his head and looked into her eyes as they drove onto the construction site. Her tummy felt light and fluttery and she swallowed.

5

____

Spencer jumped from the truck and moved to the passenger side with ease. At least his movements seemed at ease. He felt conflicted or something. Puzzled? No, that wasn't it. Defeated? Nah. He shook his head and opened the passenger door. He held his hand out for Kenna and she laid her hand on his as she exited his truck. Her hands were soft, his weren't.

She swiped her long, dark hair off her shoulders and tilted her head up to lock eyes with him. She had pretty green eyes, framed by dark thick lashes. Her lips had a layer of gloss on them and the waning daylight lit them up when they moved.

"Thank you for going with me."

"You're welcome. Let me know when you want to go back up and we'll try again."

"I don't want to keep taking you away from your work."

He grinned at her. "According to the sheriff, this is part of my work. They brought us here to stop the BRR from destroying the base and to keep the peace in town until things settle down."

Her smile faltered, but she recovered quickly and plastered on a smile. But it didn't reach her eyes.

"Okay. Thank you for your time. I'll let you know when I want to go back up there."

"Sounds good. Drive careful, Kenna."

He liked how her name rolled off his tongue. *Kenna.*

She hesitated a moment, then turned and strode to her Jeep. He watched her fluid movements as she hopped up and started the engine. She quickly buckled her seatbelt and backed from her parking spot.

"Were you successful?" He turned to Henry, who had snuck up on him.

"No."

They both watched Kenna's Jeep leave the construction site. Henry turned and clomped up the metal steps to the construction trailer, as he strode across the gravel site toward his tower and the cut wires he needed to repair so they could go home.

He pulled his tool belt from the locker near the tower and buckled it on. With a heavy sigh, he climbed the tower. They had cut the wires in two places. Nothing interesting or conspicuous about the location, just two random and close places.

While he was up there, he glanced toward the mountain to see if anyone was watching or lurking around. The BRR had been rather quiet and at least Gerard Weston, who was Craig Howard's brother-in-law, and the vice president of the BRR, had been communicating with them. If they had any more issues with the kids coming down, he'd talk to Gerard, or his son, Jasiah. Gerard wanted peace. Jasiah did as well, but they were a divided community up there. According to Gerard, it was more volatile than before, mostly because those who wanted peace were now targeted by the old-school BRR who wanted things the way they had been. Change is hard and many of them up there had never had to abide by the US laws nor those of the town of Glen Hollow.

With a heavy sigh, he climbed down the tower. It wasn't his fight or his problem, unless they made it his problem.

As he strutted along the grounds toward the construction trailer, one worker caught up to him.

"Hey, how do you know Kenna?"

He stopped and looked at the man. "I don't, really."

The man stuck out his hand. "Colt Lowe."

"Hi, Colt. Spencer Lawson."

"But I saw you drive her up the mountain."

"Yeah. I did. She had a job to do, and the sheriff asked me to help her."

"What job?"

Spencer took a deep breath and let it out slowly. "Colt, I'm not sure that you're supposed to know any of this stuff, so I'll just say she had a job and they asked me to help her."

"I went to high school with her. Back when she lived here, that is. I'm surprised to see her back in town, is all."

Spencer nodded. "I see. Well, you can ask Kenna what's going on if you like, and if she wants you to know, she'll tell you."

He hesitated, then nodded and continued on toward the trailer. He listened to the sounds behind him, though, to make sure he wasn't being followed. But he heard Colt walk toward the building he'd been working on, and Spencer let out the breath he was holding in case this turned into something else. Mostly because it was weird. Then he wondered how many people were still living here in town that knew Kenna. Likely a ton of them. People here didn't seem to leave.

Henry exited the trailer and waved to him, then strutted to his truck. It was quittin' time.

He waved in return and picked up his pace. He entered the construction trailer and checked the cameras on the computer to make sure they were working again. Pleased with himself and suddenly feeling tired, he picked up his laptop and left the trailer, locking the door behind him.

As he drove through town, he looked at Kenna's business, The Paper Trail, and now it made perfect sense to him. He chuckled. She parked her Jeep out front and he imagined her inside, her long dark hair tossed over her shoulder and her pretty fingers with the shiny fingernail polish pouring over paperwork and notes.

He took a deep breath and continued on toward the HOG, his home now. And the place where he could let out a deep breath and relax.

He pulled into the garage and grabbed his tool belt and laptop and sauntered into his sanctuary. Maya and her twin brother, Myles, sat at the counter laughing at something on a laptop when he walked in. Helissa, their cook and housekeeper, was cutting up potatoes for supper.

"Hey, everyone."

"Hi, Spencer. Did you have a good day?" Helissa asked.

"I did. How about you?"

Maya turned the laptop around, and there was a closeup of a baby. "This is Teagan Dunbar, Aidyn and Elena's baby girl."

"Oh, Elena had the baby?" He scooted closer to the monitor and stared at the little beauty. "She's tiny."

Maya laughed. "Elena doesn't think so."

He glanced at Maya and saw her grin, and the reality of what she meant hit him. "Oh. Oh, God, no, I don't want to talk about that."

Maya, Myles, and Helissa all laughed, and he felt his face burn.

6

Kiara finished her entry onto the Affidavit of Service she needed to complete regarding the service, or attempted service, on Craig Howard. They allowed three attempts per service before she had to add a fee. Her father hated adding that additional fee. He'd always prided himself on ferreting people out and getting the job done. She hoped she didn't disappoint him this time.

Saving her document, she closed the lid on her laptop and straightened up her desk. She'd gotten through filling out all the affidavits her father had in the system. She'd had him sign them at lunchtime and now she'd either emailed them out or sent them via the mail service, depending on the client's preference.

Sliding her laptop into its case, she locked the front door, turned off the lights, and strode to the back of the building and up the stairs to her apartment.

Her dad had kept it open all these years and when she came home, she stayed here. Dad's place was nice and all, but he had his way of doing things and she had hers. Plus, if she went out with friends, she didn't want to have to sneak into the house like a wayward teenager.

Unlocking the door, she stepped inside, and relief washed over her as her body relaxed. She'd done alright for today. She had organized both the old and new affidavits and implemented a new system in the office.

She gently laid her laptop on the wooden table in the kitchen. Slipping her heels off, she glanced down at the scuffs and wrinkled her nose. She rummaged through the closet in the hall that contained everything from extra towels to a toolbox on the floor to all the things in between. She found the wax paste her dad had always used to shine his shoes and grabbed a rag. Sitting on the sofa, she began applying the wax to her shoes to, at a minimum, camouflage the scuffs. At a maximum, she'd be able to wax those scuffs right off.

Her phone rang, and she laid her shoe and the wax on the coffee table and stumbled to her purse. On the fourth ring, she tapped the answer icon, "Hi. It's Kenna."

Giggling on the other end of the line made her cheeks flush hot. "Hi, Kenna, it's Lara."

"Hi, Lara. I'm sorry, I was in the other room."

"It's alright. It sounded like you were busy. I'm only calling to extend an invitation for girls' night. Shianne and I would love to have dinner and catch up. And I thought I'd ask my two new roommates, Adelaide and Maya, to join us. They don't know many people here and I thought it would help them and you to meet someone new. Plus, it's just been a long time."

She plopped on the sofa. "You have roommates? I thought you got married."

Lara's laugh was genuine. "I guess that did sound weird. We have roommates. Tate's company remodeled the old sewing factory on the edge of town into a beautiful home, office, and working facility. We all live out here."

"Oh, wow. I didn't know. I only just got into town a couple of nights ago and I haven't had the chance to get around and see any of the changes. Other than seeing you at the bakery this morning, I've been nowhere else."

"Well, we don't have to do it tonight, but what if we plan for tomorrow night? You won't have to cook, and we don't have to make it a late night. I still get up early to bake, so let's just make it dinner and a couple of drinks."

"Tomorrow sounds great. You'll need to pick the place, since I'm not sure what's still here."

"Sounds good. Let's head out to the Broken Barrel and have heavy, greasy bar food."

"Ugh, my pants just pinched me."

Lara laughed, and she joined her. It felt good to laugh. "I'll see you tomorrow night. How about five-thirty?"

Kenna nodded. "Five-thirty at the Broken Barrel. See you then."

She put her phone on the sofa next to her and her stomach tightened. Colt Lowe probably still lived in town. It was unlikely he'd ever leave here. She picked her phone up and tapped Lara's number. She bit her bottom lip as she listened to the rings.

"Hey, Kenna, that was fast, what's up?"

"I just wondered if you knew if Colt Lowe was still in town."

Lara hesitated for far longer than was comfortable. "He is."

"Does he hang out at the Broken Barrel?"

"Pardon my nosiness, but you aren't hoping to meet up with him, are you?"

"Oh, God, no. I don't want to see him."

"Whew. The last I heard, someone had kicked him out of the Broken Barrel."

"Fighting?"

"Yep. And threatening to kill Chesson Ward. He still owns the Broken Barrel."

"He threatened to kill him? Was he drunk?"

"Not really. He'd had a couple beers, but he was just in one of his surly moods."

Kenna sat back on the sofa and stared out the tall windows at the far end of her living room. The sun was setting, though it was staying light longer these days.

"Do you see him much?"

"Not too much. He only comes into the bakery when he has to pick up something for his mom. Then, he's usually nice enough."

"Okay. Thank you for letting me know this stuff. I don't want to run into him if I can help it."

"You're welcome. I heard he's engaged to Ami Pearson."

"From high school? That Ami Pearson?"

"Yes." She could hear Lara moving around. Then a door closed. "She's always had a crush on him. Throughout school, when you were dating him, she bemoaned the fact that he didn't even know she existed."

"You're kidding!" Kenna sat up and shoved her hair off her shoulder. "I never knew that."

"Well, you were working or with Colt. The rest of us had to listen to her complain. I suspect we'll still have to hear her complain, though it will be for the reasons we all know, and she seems oblivious to."

Gathering her hair together at her nape, she rotated her head. "Yeah."

7

Spencer pulled his phone from his back pocket and tapped Aidyn's number.

"Hey, there, what's up?"

Spencer chuckled. "Not much. I hear you live in a house with two women."

"Good lord, that I do."

"She's beautiful. Congratulations."

"Thank you." Cooing and little sounds came over the phone. "She's unbelievable."

"Everyone doing okay?" Spencer tried imagining his burly friend holding something as small as a baby, but the picture wouldn't come.

Aidyn chuckled. "Everyone is great. Teagan sleeps like a champ, almost six hours at a crack, which we're thrilled about."

He chuckled. "That's fantastic. Where did you get the name Teagan?"

Aidyn's voice sounded unfamiliar. Like he was in a state of disbelief. "My dad's grandma's name was Teagan.

He was telling us about her one night and we both loved the name."

"It's a noble name. I'm looking forward to meeting her, Aid. Congratulations again." Spencer heard a little squeak of a sound, and Aidyn cooed. Spencer chuckled. "Dammit man, you've been domesticated."

"I know it. But I'm not unhappy about it."

He nodded and grinned. "Take care, man. Send my regards to Elena."

"Will do Spence. It means a lot that you called."

Spencer scoffed, as if he wouldn't. "Shut up."

He ended the call and pocketed his phone. He left his room to head out to the shooting range and met Henry leaving his room.

"Hey, did I see you talking to Colt Lowe at the site?"

His brows furrowed. "Yeah, you know him?"

"Only that he has a temper, and it's wild. I've not witnessed it, but it's a legend around the site."

"Why do they keep someone like him on, then?"

Henry shrugged. "Great question for Baxter."

He nodded and moved toward the back of the house and the shooting range. His shoulders felt stiff, and he still had that nagging heaviness weighing on him. Damned if he knew what it was. His mouth watered as he entered the kitchen. "Supper smells good, Helissa."

She turned from the stove and smiled at him. "Roast pork, potatoes, carrots, and apple pie for dessert."

"I'm gonna weigh a ton when I get back home."

She laughed, and he felt joy at the sound.

He continued on through the garage and to the shooting range Aidyn's parents had set up for them. It was a blessing having one on site. They'd always had one back home in Lynyrd Station and it was one of those things you got used to but thought little about. When they first got here, they set up a temporary range at the construction site. What they found was they seldom used it because there was always something going on. Plus, after a few months, the rubber and sand they shot into had to be cleaned out. That was a tremendous pain.

As the lights flickered on, he pulled his practice gun from its shelf and set about loading the magazine and checking his gun over. Donning his protective eyewear and noise-cancelling earbuds, he stepped up to the shooting lane, added a target to the clip and pushed it back to fifteen feet.

The first squeeze of the trigger he felt tight. Rolling his head on his shoulders, he inhaled deeply and slowly released it. Hold, aim, shoot, breathe. Repeat.

His first magazine of thirteen rounds emptied, and he refilled. Thirteen more and he'd call it a day.

He felt his phone buzz in his pocket. Laying his gun in its case, he pulled his earplugs out and chuckled when he saw the name on his phone.

"Hey, Mom."

Her laughter on the end of the line relaxed his shoulders.

"Hey, sweetheart, how are you?"

He grinned and leaned on the table with his butt. "What's up?"

"I miss you and wanted to touch base. How are you?"

"I'm good. We've gotten a small reprieve here from the BRR. But it looks like not a complete reprieve."

"They sure are stubborn."

He laughed. "That they are." He inhaled and let a breath out. "How's Dad? How are you?"

"Dad's good. Dani's getting married."

"She is? Wow, to Rhys, or did she find someone else along the way?"

"Spencer! You make your sister sound like a tramp."

"I did not. I don't think she's a tramp at all. Last time I spoke to her, though, she seemed hesitant about Rhys."

She was hesitant about Rhys, but she said Rhys feared her family. Tough shit, he'd have to deal if they were getting married.

"She told me Rhys is afraid of us."

He laughed. "Yeah, that just popped into my head, too. Too bad. If they get married, he'll need to deal and if he does anything to hurt her, he'll know genuine fear for sure."

"Spencer! Don't go scaring him off."

"There's no better way to find out if he'll stick around than to make him work for it."

His mom was quiet for a long time, then she burst out laughing. His mom was a tough cookie. She was beautiful and smart, too. But she wasn't a shrinking violet at all.

"That's true!"

Spencer stood and paced the floor a few steps in one direction, then turned and paced back.

His mom's laughter faded. "Dad and I are thinking about making the trip down to see you. When is a good time?"

"You can come anytime, Mom. We have plenty of room here and we'd all love to see you both."

"Okay. I'll talk to your dad, and we'll plan some time to visit. I miss you, Spence."

"I miss you too, Mom. Tell Dad hello. I love you both."

"We love you so much, honey. Call your sister."

The call ended and his heart felt heavier than before.

Maybe that was it. He was homesick. He'd spent a year stationed in Afghanistan and he wasn't as homesick as he felt right now. Of course, in Afghanistan, he was constantly ducking bullets and dodging land mines.

Kenna sat across the table from her father. She held her bottom lip between her teeth as she stared at him. His color was off. He looked rather gray, and his movements were slow. But he'd insisted on coming into the office today. In about five minutes, she was calling her mom to come and pick him up. He needed to rest. As stubborn as he was, she was putting her foot down. But it's what had made him a good process server. He always got the job done. And that's how she learned the business.

Okay, and what about this one? Did you effect service to Brookswood?" She held a work order out to him.

"Yes, I believe I did. Look in my notebook, Kenna. I have it written down."

She skimmed the pages in the spiral notebook her father carried with him everywhere he went. He jotted down what he'd done, where he went, and who he served every moment of each day. He even scribbled in what he had for lunch along the way.

The office phone rang, and it reminded her to call and

cancel the office phone. She'd answer it on her cell phone. When she went back to Houston, her father could answer on his cell phone. There was no sense in paying out good money when they didn't have to.

She answered, "Paper Trail."

"Good morning. This is Francesca Smith from Smith Squared. I have papers to be served today, if possible."

"Of course. Hi, Ms. Smith, this is Kenna Lawrence, Howie's daughter."

"Oh, I'm sorry I didn't recognize your voice, Kenna. Are you back and working with your dad?"

Kenna took a deep breath. She was getting this question a lot. "I'm here helping for a bit. I'll be heading back to Houston when all is well here." She purposely avoided looking at her father.

"I'm sorry. I heard your dad wasn't feeling well. Is he better?"

She quickly studied her father now. He had pulled the notebook toward him and was moving a shaking finger down the page as he looked through his notes.

"Yes. Thank you for asking. I can be over in about a half hour to pick up the papers. Where do they need to be served?"

"Craig Howard and Kent Bennit."

Her heart hit her stomach with a thud. She still hadn't served yesterday's papers. But Spencer had said each day was different, so maybe today would be that day.

"Okay. I'll see you in a half hour."

She waited until Ms. Smith hung up, then she replaced the receiver into the cradle on the ancient-looking phone. At least it was a push-button, but still.

Slogging back to the table, she sat and let her breath

out slowly. "What was that all about?" her father softly asked.

"Attorney Smith has some papers to be served today."

"That so?" He picked up a pen and underlined something in his notebook. Even his lines were shaky.

She pulled her phone off the table and texted her mom.

"Dad needs to come home."

She saw the dots dancing before the message.

"I'll be right there."

She inhaled deeply and looked at the passages her father underlined in his notebook. She made her own notes on her laptop so she could complete the Affidavits of Service when her father dropped the pen and sat back in his chair.

Fear crawled through her as she stared at his body, which seemed frozen. "Daddy?"

He didn't move, and she stood. Leaning over, she touched his cheek lightly. "Daddy?"

The front door opened, and she whipped her head around. "Mama, Daddy isn't moving or answering me." She swallowed the panic that clenched her throat.

Her mom rushed over. "Howie, open your eyes."

His faded blue eyes opened, though he didn't seem to recognize either of them. Her mom shook her dad's shoulder, and he blinked a few times before spitting out, "Stop shaking me, Niya."

"Well, you weren't responding again, Howie."

Again? Kenna swallowed the dread that clawed up her spine.

He shook his head slightly. "I'm tired. I want to go home."

Her mom helped her dad stand, but Kenna's heart wouldn't stop racing.

"Mama, maybe you should call the ambulance and get Daddy to the hospital."

"I'm not going to the damned hospital. Whole blasted town will know everything about me five minutes after I land there. Then business will drop off."

"Daddy, business isn't more important than your health."

"Says the girl who traipsed off to Houston the second she could." He bit back.

"I didn't…" She stopped at the glare her mother shot her.

Huffing out a breath and feeling complete defeat, she stepped to the other side of her father and put her arm under his to help him walk to the car. As they neared the door, her father whispered, "Kenna, look out and make sure no one's out there looking."

She did as he asked, knowing how important it was for him not to appear weak to anyone in town. Stepping onto the front porch, she looked around and the town seemed rather peaceful.

"It's all clear, Daddy."

She moved to his side again, and he waved her off. Glancing behind her father's back toward her mom, she received a slight shake of the head, and they stepped past her and out to the front porch. Her mom had parked to the side so the passenger door was closest to the door so her father could slip into the car with minimal exposure.

"Proud, stubborn mule," she whispered.

She waited until her mom got into the driver's seat and waved, then she closed the door so the heat wouldn't have time to warm up the whole inside of the office.

Inhaling a deep, cleansing breath, she gathered up the papers she and her dad had been working on when the front door opened again.

Her mom hustled in. "Daddy wants his notebook. Says he'll underline all the important things you need to prepare for the affidavits."

"Mama, shouldn't he rest?"

"Kenna, he won't rest if we don't give him his damned notebook."

"Wait!" Kenna scooped up the notebook and pulled her phone up. She scanned pages quickly with the scanning app so she could continue to get the paperwork caught up.

With a frown, she handed it to her mom. Her mom kissed her cheek, then skipped toward the door in a hurry to get back before her father tried coming back in.

Kenna locked the door behind her mom, hustled upstairs to change into jeans and tennis shoes and a lightweight t-shirt. She'd try a different approach toward Craig today to see if that worked any better. Couldn't hurt.

As soon as she'd changed, she hustled out the back door, and ran next door to Smith Squared to pick up her papers.

The law office was neat, clean, and incredibly quiet. The Smiths had updated their furniture with a modern mahogany desk and richly upholstered chairs, creating the upscale atmosphere they were known for.

The receptionist smiled at her, "Hi there, Kenna. Attorney Smith has the paperwork right here for you."

Jessie had been a freshman when Kenna was a senior in high school. She didn't look like she'd aged much at all. Still slightly plump, with a cute dimple on her right cheek.

"Thank you, Jessie. How are you doing?"

"I'm good. I've got two babies now and trying to lose all that weight. You look fantastic. How are you?"

"I'm good. Trying to catch up with all the comings and goings around here."

"I understand that. Did you know Colt is engaged to Ami Pearson?"

Ah, so she was trying to see her reaction. Likely still friends with Ami. "I heard that. If I recall correctly, she always had a crush on him. Good for them."

She smiled brightly and noticed the twitch Jessie's lips made. Kenna bit the inside of her cheek to keep from smiling. Pegged her!

"Yes, I think the wedding will be this summer. Will you be around for it?"

Ah, this was typical. Gossip. The second she was out the door, Jessie would call Ami. "I'm not really sure if I'll still be here, and to be honest, I'll bet neither of them would be comfortable with me around. So, I'll hang back and let them have their big day. Every bride and groom should have that, don't you think?"

"Oh, sure. I mean, yes, of course."

Kenna picked up the folder with her paperwork inside and smiled brightly. "You have a great day, Jessie. I've got to get these papers served."

She turned quickly and strode out the door, her back straight, her ponytail swishing and her pride intact. Nice.

Outside, she looked up the mountain and sent up a silent prayer that Craig was in a better mood today.

She hopped in her Jeep, with both sets of paperwork to serve on Craig, and headed toward the mountain road closest to her office. Perhaps there would be different BRR members guarding this road and she'd be able to get past them.

9

Spencer strolled along the newly laid footings at the construction site, calculating how the walls would change their visibility and how he'd need to change his cameras. He twisted his head to see the camera pointing at this spot, then turned toward the camera on the far left of the site, pointing this direction. He needed two more cameras.

Baxter Fenshaw sidled up behind him. "Well, what do you think?"

"Two more cameras. When will the walls be up?"

"Tomorrow. Thursday at the latest."

"Okay. I'll bring the cameras with me tomorrow. No need to install them until I can see the walls and where to position them."

Spencer moved toward the north side of the footings. "There'll be one door here?" He pointed to the other break in the footings. "One there." Then pointed to the back of the building. "And one there?"

"Yes. This building is the armory, so we'll need cameras inside, too."

"Okay. I'll work with the security company to ensure we're all together with our equipment."

Baxter rubbed his chin with his left hand. "Did you find out anything about the kid from yesterday?"

Spencer shook his head and mentally told himself not to slouch. He felt sheepish about that incident. "No. Haven't seen hide nor hair of him. I've checked all the camera footage, and he seemed to appear out of nowhere."

"I'm guessing it was a prank. Summer football training is starting at the high school and my gut tells me it was a freshman initiation prank."

"They do that here?"

Baxter laughed a hearty belly laugh. "Oh, they do that. Every freshman, every year, has to do something considered dangerous or daring."

Spencer turned to face Baxter head on. "What did you have to do your freshman year?"

Baxter shook his head slowly. "I'm not proud, know that. I had to hot-wire a used car from the dealership in town. It's no longer here, but I hot-wired a Cougar and drove it to the back of the old sewing factory where you live. Cops were all over town looking for that damned car."

Spencer's mouth hung open for a minute, before he realized his action and snapped it closed. "You're shitting me?"

"I am not." Baxter shook his head again. His beefy shoulders shaking as he laughed.

"Did you get caught?"

"Nope."

"No shit?"

Footsteps approached. "No shit what?"

He glanced at Henry, who stopped near them, his brows pinched together and lifted.

Baxter sighed. "I hot-wired a car when I was young and dumb."

Henry stared, his mouth hanging open. When he finally closed his mouth, he shook his head. "If someone had bet me a hundred dollars that you were a rebel when you were younger, I would have taken that bet. You're the straightest arrow I know."

Baxter laughed. "We'll leave it at that."

He turned and sauntered back toward the construction crew as they began to clean up for the day. Spencer turned to Henry. "What's up?"

"Tate called. Casper wants a meeting. Tonight at five-thirty."

"Okay. I'll head right out of here after the construction crew leaves and the cameras are in place."

"Sounds good. I'm heading out now. I'm on grocery pick-up duty."

Spencer chuckled and slapped Henry on the back. "You're always on grocery pick-up duty."

"Don't I know it. Helissa thinks I'm only good for picking up heavy things."

Spencer laughed as his friend's feet scraped the ground as he trudged toward his truck. He glanced up to see Colt Lowe staring at him. The fine hairs on the back of his neck prickled as he held Colt's gaze. There was something akin to evil in that man's face, but he couldn't quite put his finger on it. He'd steer clear of him, but he'd be damned if he'd back down from Colt. He lifted a hand to wave and pasted a smile on his face.

Finally, Colt looked away and walked toward the parking area.

The sun glinting off a vehicle up the BRR road caught his eye.

Kenna's Jeep cleared the trees and brush, and he swore as he jogged toward the front of the lot. She was driving too fast and sped into the lot, slamming on her brakes just before hitting the construction trailer.

Colt beat him to her Jeep and flung open her door.

He heard her scream, "Get the fuck away from me! You hear me? Get away."

"I'm not doing shit to you, you crazy bitch."

Spencer ran full speed to Kenna's Jeep. When he got there, he yelled, "What the hell is going on?"

Colt turned and pierced him with the scariest glare he'd ever seen. Spencer shook his head and pushed past him to Kenna. That's when his stomach roiled and his heartbeat raced faster than a Ferrari on the Autobahn.

"Kenna, what the hell..."

She looked into his eyes, tears spilling from hers. His eyes widened at her beautiful, bruised, cut, and dirty face. Without thinking, he reached in, sliding his left arm under her legs and his right arm behind her waist, and pulled her from her Jeep. He carried her into the construction trailer as she wept in his arms.

Colt followed behind him, and he whirled around, Kenna still in his arms. "Get out of here. Now."

"I want to see her injuries."

Kenna cried out. "You've seen plenty of my injuries, Colt. Get away from me."

Spencer's jaw tightened, and his stomach rolled. The door swung open and Baxter filled the doorway.

"Colt, get out of here."

"But, I'm just..."

"Get. Out. Now." Baxter clipped.

Colt stomped out swearing and muttering something about this not being over and Spencer's jaw tightened once again. He'd find out later what this was all about.

He gently set Kenna on the softest chair in the trailer, which wasn't much more than a padded metal folding chair. Kneeling in front of her, he looked into her eyes. "Where are you hurt the most, Kenna?"

She sniffed and opened her mouth to speak, but nothing came out. He pulled his phone from his pocket and tapped Adelaide's picture.

"Hey, are you on your way back?" she asked. "Helissa said supper is almost ready."

Spencer's stomach twisted as he watched Kenna's face. "No. I need you to come here. They've beaten Kenna Lawrence. Bring your medical kit."

He ended the call without another word and dropped his phone on the floor near his knees.

"Kenna, honey, can you tell me where the pain is worst?"

She swallowed and lifted her hand to the side of her right eye. He saw the bruising spreading and forming, and the swelling was already nearly twice the size of her left eye. He feared she had a fractured eye socket. Addy could tell better than he.

"Did Craig do this?"

Tears streamed down her cheeks, and he waited in fear that the wailing was trying to burst free. All she did was barely nod her head.

"Why did you go up there alone?"

She stared at him but didn't say a word.

10

———

Her heart beat so hard it almost hurt. She could feel the pulsing in her neck and the throbbing in her face with each quick beat. Spencer assessed her face. He held her hand as he ran his other hand up her arms, looking for any signs of injury.

Gently, he laid her right hand on her lap as he slowly lifted her right leg. But he watched her face as he did to see if she felt pain. When she didn't cry out or wince, he smiled at her. He was handsome. Incredibly handsome. This close to him, she could see his dark thick lashes surrounding grass green eyes. She swallowed down the envy. Thick lashes with no makeup—every woman's dream.

Spencer lifted her left leg slowly, watching her face. She swallowed and her heart didn't slow. In fact, it sped up. He smelled like spices and citrus and something she couldn't identify.

Tears spilled down her cheeks and heat raced up her body as she realized what she must look like at this moment to him.

"How about your ribs Kenna? Do they hurt?"

Her right hand laid against her rib cage and she pressed in. He grinned at her then and whispered, "Take a slow, deep breath, honey."

Honey? Honey! Wow, that sounded so nice. She did as he asked and winced slightly.

"Show me where it hurts."

Her left hand laid against her left rib cage and he let out a breath. "I'm going to lift your shirt slightly to see if you have bruising. I'll be careful not to lift too high."

He stared into her eyes and she finally whispered, "Okay."

He gently lifted the left side of her t-shirt up and stopped. His fingers were gentle when he touched her. Softly pressing around the area where that jerk had kicked her.

The trailer door opened and soft footsteps entered behind her. She swallowed and closed her eyes. At least Spencer was here, and where did Baxter go? Hopefully, he made Colt go home.

Spencer smiled at the person behind her and moved over to her right side.

He looked into her eyes. "Kenna, honey, this is my friend Adelaide. We call her Addy. She's our team medic. She's here to look at your injuries. Will you let her?"

She swallowed, and it felt like she had a pound of dust in her mouth. "Yes." It came out as a croak, and she tried swallowing again. "Yes."

He hurried to the refrigerator and pulled out a bottle of water. He twisted the cap and held it out to her. Her hands shook as she wrapped her fingers around the bottle. Her fingers touched his, and she felt shivers run up her fingers. He smiled at her and she struggled to look away.

Lifting the bottle to her lips, she swallowed down several gulps of water and closed her eyes as the cold liquid slid down her throat. Spencer reached forward and took the bottle of water from her and replaced the cap.

Addy knelt down in front of her and her beautiful brown shiny eyes assessed her face first. "Kenna, can you tell me where you're hurting the worst?"

She lifted her hand to the right side of her face again and Addy's smart, concerned eyes examined the area. "I'm going to touch you to see if I can feel anything. I'm not trying to cause you harm, but you may feel some pain. Just let me know when it's too much."

"Okay."

She closed her eyes as Addy's gentle fingers felt around her eye and into her temple. She probed across her eyebrow and down the bridge of her nose. "I don't feel anything broken. But maybe we should take you into the hospital for X-rays."

"No. Please. My dad will be so upset. If I don't get better in a few days, I'll go in, but I don't think anything is broken. I'm feeling bruised and battered and tired. Maybe I need to go home and lay down." Her voice shook, and she hated she felt weak. Her eyes welled with tears and she swallowed. "I'm just tired," she whispered.

Addy dabbed a cloth near her eyes and smiled at her. She was beautiful, petite with long dark hair she'd braided and flipped over her right shoulder. Little curls escaped the braid and framed her face. Her teeth were incredibly white and straight and right now Kenna felt so ugly and beaten and worn that she sobbed. Her hands flew to her face, and she covered her ugliness as Addy stroked her back and softly whispered close to her ear, "You've been through a lot today, and you're experiencing an adrenaline crash right now. It's normal and expected and believe it or not, crying is cleansing your eyes out, so this is all good."

She let it out. Addy handed her the cloth she had dabbed near her eyes, and she gripped it between her hands and cried into it. Addy continued to rub her back. She tried taking a deep breath and cried out as it hurt. Addy's hands froze, and she heard Spencer gently explain.

"She has an injury on her left rib area."

Addy gently lifted her t-shirt, and Kenna swiped under her eyes with the cloth, horrified when she saw all her mascara on the cloth. It had likely been running down her face. Her cheeks burned hot.

Addy's fingers were gentle as she moved around the injury. "It looks like a contusion. If you try slowly to inhale, can you?"

She sat back against the back of the chair, now embarrassed to look at Spencer. She inhaled slowly and let it out slowly. It pinched, but not more than that.

"Okay. Good. I don't think anything is broken."

"He kicked me there." Her lips trembled, but she didn't burst out crying this time.

"Yeah. You'll have a nice bruise there for a few days."

Her eyes darted to Spencer, who still kneeled near her, watching and assessing. He held her bottle of water and she reached a hand out to it. He grinned as he handed it to her, and she drank down a few more swallows of water. The cooling was still satisfying, but not as cold as it had been prior.

"Kenna, you'll need someone to stay with you overnight to make sure you don't have a concussion. We should monitor you for headaches, dizziness, ringing in the ears, loss of balance, and sensitivity to light and sounds. Do you have someone who can stay with you or somewhere you can stay where there will be someone with you?"

She closed her eyes. She would not go to her parents' home. Would not. She wasn't even going to tell them about this. Her girlfriends from high school all had kids. She didn't want to go to anyone's house looking like this. So, she lied. "I can have my mom stay with me tonight."

Her eyes darted from Spencer to Addy, and she swallowed. She hated lying. But she'd just monitor herself and set her alarm often to get up and make sure she didn't have a concussion.

"Okay. Let me clean up some of these cuts and bandage them, then you can go home and lie down."

11

Henderson kept swaying back and forth and recalled that her father had been unwell. So why would her mom choose to leave him and stay with Kenna? He pulled a metal chair close and helped as Addy cleaned her injuries and bandaged her up. She sat straight and barely moved as Addy applied ointment and dressing. She only winced twice, and he watched as she bit her lips at others. Addy cleaned the cuts on her arms and applied the ointment. These seemed to be sensitive, but not as bad as the cuts on her face and above her eyes.

Addy cleaned up her empty gauze packages and applicators, and he watched Kenna. She was stoic. And brave. Maybe too brave. But she was beautiful. And she had a lot of secrets. She didn't say she had them. He got that feeling in his gut that she had them. Given her profession and the confidentiality she needed to provide to her clients, he assumed that seeped into her private life, too.

Addy closed up her medical bag and stood. "Kenna, why don't you let us drive you home?"

"I can drive myself." It came out funny because her

bottom lip was now swollen. She touched it with her right hand and her nose wrinkled.

He looked up at Addy. "I've got this. I'll make sure she gets home."

Addy waved to him. "I'll see you back at the HOG."

He nodded. "Thanks, Addy."

Kenna's eyes rounded. At least as much as they could round with the swelling.

He held his hand out. "Need help standing?"

"No. I'm good." She tried, wobbled, and fell hard on the chair. She let out an "oof" when she landed. He saw her swallow and her right hand wrapped around her left rib cage.

He stepped closer. "Take my hand."

He held his hand out to her, and she stared at it for a moment, then rested her right hand in his right. He closed his fingers around hers and stiffened so she'd have something solid to help her stand. She had to be getting sore as the adrenaline left her body. It would be a rough night.

She exhaled and struggled up to a standing position. A slight grunt sounded from somewhere deep inside. Once standing, she stood stock-still and he let her get her bearings. Holding her hand was nice. It fit in his hand. He liked the feel of her warm skin against his. He marveled at the size difference between his hand and hers.

She inhaled deeply. Slowly. Then she took a step away from the chair and he heard her intake of breath. She took another, and he knew her pain had increased.

"Let me drive you home tonight. We'll come back and get your Jeep tomorrow or I can have one of my teammates come and get it and I'll take them home."

"I can drive."

"It's a stick shift, isn't it?"

"Yeah."

"Kenna?" he snapped.

She stopped and turned her head. "Honey, let me drive you home. Your eyes are swollen. You can barely move. You're sore. I'll get you home safely. Get you some ibuprofen, maybe some hot tea, and you can get some rest while you wait for your mom to get to your place."

She took another stubborn step and winced. He moved in front of her and looked into her eyes. "Let me help you."

She swallowed, and he saw the indecision in her eyes. Her eyes darted across the room to the wall and then back to him. He grinned and squeezed her hand gently. "Come on, let's get you home."

She seemed to feel relieved she didn't have to decide and allowed him to help her out of the trailer. The descent down the three metal steps seemed difficult for her, but she never complained. He just followed her lead with the speed at which they moved. Which was slower than a damned turtle crossing the road.

Once on the ground, they dragged along toward their vehicles and he moved her toward his. She looked up into his eyes and he smiled. "It'll be fine. Where are your keys?"

"In the Jeep. I didn't take them out."

"Okay. I'll get them in a minute." It would be many more minutes, for sure.

Their forward progress was slow, painfully slow. But they finally made it to his truck, and she froze. He opened the door and the power running boards dropped and he saw her relax.

"Okay. First foot on the board. Step up. Hand on my shoulder for support and slide yourself onto the seat."

She followed his instructions and finally got herself into the seat. He pulled her seatbelt around her body and clicked it into place. His shoulder brushed her breasts.

Perv. He chastised himself for thinking thoughts not entirely pure as he helped an injured woman into his truck. A beautiful, injured woman. An incredibly beautiful woman. He let out a breath at the direction of his thoughts and stood back.

"Are you okay?"

She nodded slowly, and he grinned. "I'm going to park your Jeep over there." He pointed to the other vehicles. "Then I'll be right back."

"Okay," she all but whispered.

He stalked over to her Jeep, not feeling very proud of himself, but, well, what could he do? She didn't know the direction of his thoughts.

After parking her Jeep, he made his way to his truck and climbed inside behind the steering wheel. Backing from his parking space, he turned to look at her. "Where do you live?"

Her eyes landed on his, and she licked her lips. *Damn.*

"I live above The Paper Trail."

His brows furrowed, then he shrugged and headed off toward her home.

He stopped in front of the building and she whispered, "Can you park around back? I don't want anyone seeing me like this."

"Of course." He pulled around the back of the building and helped her down from the truck, which seemed much worse than getting into it. The few minutes it took to get this far seemed to have made her stiff and likely the pain was rolling over her in waves.

He'd get her situated, and she'd get some relief soon.

Finally reaching the top step to her apartment, she let out the breath she'd been holding. She'd known pain in her life, but it had been years and she didn't remember it being quite like this.

Spencer took her keys and unlocked her apartment door. She'd always been neat so there wasn't fear of undergarments lying around, but that first impression meant something to her. He quickly glanced around the room and helped her through the door by holding her hand, his other hand on her hip, and leading her forward.

Her small kitchen opened to the living room. The vaulted ceilings up here made the place seem much larger than it was. The gigantic windows in the living room let the sunshine in and made the entire apartment cozy and happy. That's one reason she wanted to stay here. She enjoyed it up here.

He led her to the sofa, at a right angle to the windows so she could look out.

His body was firm and his support meant everything right now. She lowered herself onto the sofa and leaned back. Finally, letting out a sigh that she could rest a bit, she laid her head back and closed her eyes.

"Do you like tea or coffee?"

Her eyes flung open and landed on his. She swallowed and tried sitting up but winced when pain sliced through her body from her ribs. Her breath caught and Spencer sat next to her on the sofa and gently laid his hand on her shoulder.

"Why don't you relax and let me help you? Where do you keep whatever it is you like to drink?"

She let her head roll toward him, and she smiled. Though it likely didn't look like a smile. The swelling in her bottom lip tightened her mouth and pulled when she tried, so she stopped smiling and blinked rapidly to keep the tears from flowing again. She should have been cried out by now.

"I like tea. I have bags in the cupboard above the sink. I have a teakettle on the stove."

"Great. I'll be back with your tea soon. How about ibuprofen? Where will I find that?"

Lifting her arm to point down the hallway to her left, she softly replied, "Bathroom. Medicine cabinet."

He stood and disappeared down the hallway. She heard the cabinet door open and close and the music of ibuprofen pills dancing along each other as he tipped the bottle toward his hand. She closed her eyes as fatigue washed over her.

The sofa dipped and her eyes flew open. Spencer appeared in her line of sight, and though her brain was fuzzy, she remembered him coming home with her. She moved to sit up straight, and pain sliced through her body.

"Ouch." she cried out.

He leaned forward and held his hand out with two ibuprofen tablets in his palm. He handed her a glass of water and nodded to a plate with saltine crackers on it.

"Take these, nibble on the crackers while I make you some tea."

The sofa moved and her eyes flew open once again. Spencer lifted a warm cup of tea to her. "Sorry, it is only warm. I didn't want to hurt your mouth more than it already is."

She struggled to sit up straight, pain slicing through her body, but she wrapped her hands around the warm cup, and sipped the hot liquid. Her icy fingers shook. She glanced to her right for the blanket that usually laid along the arm of the sofa. It wasn't there, so she tilted her head to look beyond Spencer to see if it was there. He grinned and sat back. "Looking for something?"

"My blanket."

His brows furrowed slightly, then he looked over the arm of the sofa and pulled her blanket up from the floor.

"I may have pushed this over when I sat down."

He opened it up and spread it out over her lap. Then he stood. "Why don't you rest for a bit?"

"How long was I asleep?"

"About twenty minutes."

"Oh." Sipping more of the warm tea, she handed him the cup and pulled the blankets up to her chin.

Spencer bent and lifted her legs and laid them on the sofa. "Get comfortable. I'll get you another blanket to warm you and pillows to prop up your head."

She breathed through the pain as she moved, and settled herself on the sofa. For the first time in a few hours, she relaxed. She blinked a few times, then she didn't blink again for some time.

———

Warmth. Ah, she finally felt warm and snug and wrapped in a cocoon and safe and it all felt so good.

Soft breathing near her ear made her eyes fly open and her own breathing halted as she tried to get her bearings. Fear rose inside her, but she forced it down. She was wrapped in a man's arms. She was in her bedroom. In her bed. The sun had gone down, a while ago by the looks of it.

She felt the pain shoot up her ribcage as she lifted the covers. Blowing out a breath, she moved the arm wrapped around her waist and pushed herself up with her right arm.

Spencer rolled slightly, then sat up. His hands swiped down his face, then he turned to stare at her. "How do you feel? Do you need more ibuprofen?"

"How did we get in here?"

He blinked. Those impossible lashes captured her attention. The light from the hallway filtered in enough that she could see clearly.

"I carried you."

"Why?"

"You were freezing. Shivering. I laid a couple more blankets on you, but you didn't warm. I picked you up and carried you in here so I could use my body heat to help warm you. You settled down then." He lifted his arm and looked at his watch. "About four hours ago."

"I've been sleeping for four hours?" Her head spun. She didn't remember him picking her up. Carrying her to her room or crawling in behind her. "Did I talk?"

"You said thank you."

"Is that all?"

"I think so. Something about feeling safe. But you were mumbling."

"I don't mumble."

He chuckled, and she stared. His smile reached his eyes. His lips were full and when they lifted in happiness, like right now, he was a sight. A wonderful sight.

"You do. You did last night anyway."

She quickly raised her head and immediately regretted it. She raised her right hand to hold her head and felt the pain as she touched it. Spencer rolled and got up on the other side of the bed, while she let out a lengthy groan.

"I'll get you more ibuprofen and some fresh tea."

"It's okay. Don't bother."

"Kenna, I know you're used to being alone. I get it. Believe me. But I'm here and taking care of you and I've gotten my ass kicked several times. Enough to know you need painkillers, something to drink them down with, and maybe an ice pack for your swelling. How about you not argue every time I try to help and just let me do it?"

Well, now she just felt stupid and ungrateful. "I'm sorry."

He left the room, and she heard the bathroom cabinet open, the pills in the bottle as he tilted it, then the cabinet close. His footsteps down her hallway were even and soft as he moved toward her kitchen. For such a big guy, he moved easily. Her small apartment must feel like a shoebox to him. But she loved it up here.

She huffed out a breath as she slowly stood. She was sore from head to toe. The punch she took stretched every muscle she had. Tensing up didn't help.

Sliding one foot forward, then the next slowly, she got

to the bathroom. She locked the door and, as slow as a turtle, she pushed her pants and panties down enough that she could use the toilet. Easing herself down was painful. Standing up afterwards was more so. She'd ease up on the tea for a bit.

She pushed the lever to flush the toilet, then moved to the sink to wash her hands. She gasped when she looked in the mirror. Hideous. She was hideous. Her right eye was swollen, and colorful with hues of red, and purple. The white of her eye was red. A large bandage over her eyebrow filled in the rest of the look.

There was dirt on her face and smeared mascara still under her eyes. The cut on her bottom lip had bled during her sleep and a clot of blood crusted over it.

Turning to the small closet behind the bathroom door, she reached in for a washcloth. The water warmed in the faucet before she wet the washcloth. Squeezing the water from it, but not completely, she dabbed at the dirt on her face and cleared away the mascara that smudged her face. She rinsed and held the wet cloth over her bottom lip to remove the streak of dried blood, but only gently dabbed around the scab of dried blood as to not open the cut again.

Looking over her arms, she saw the cuts and abrasions from falling on the ground and the rocks gouging into her flesh. She remembered feeling it, but being so afraid it didn't register what was happening. She thought he was going to kill her.

After she'd cleaned both arms and as much of her face as she could handle right now, she left the bathroom and shuffled to her bedroom. Spencer was waiting for her at the foot of her bed.

"Are you alright?"

"Why didn't you tell me I looked like a monster?"

"You don't."

"Please. I scared myself in there."

He grinned at her, and her heart fluttered. It fluttered! She shuffled past him and sat on the edge of her bed. The two tablets and a warm cup of tea on the bedside table greeted her, and she gratefully took the tablets and sipped her tea. Lying back, she pulled the covers up to her chin.

Spencer stood and stared down at her. "Are you okay now?"

"Yes. Thank you."

He nodded and left the room. She felt bad about that. She felt safe with him around, and she kind of liked him. He differed from anyone she'd ever known.

She heard the sofa squeak as he laid down on it and she felt sad. Here he was taking care of her and he had to sleep on the couch. But inviting him back in here seemed wrong.

Then she heard the loud pipes of a truck driving past outside. Her clock said ten o'clock, and she figured the teens were out goofing off again. That was the last thought she had before drifting off.

13

The black truck drove past for the third time, and Spencer grew irritated. He sat up and watched out the living room windows. He hid in the dark, but the bright moonlight outside made it rather easy to see the comings and goings on the county road below. A few cars zipped by, no one he recognized and certainly nothing concerning. He stood and stretched, then walked to the kitchen and looked out of the window. This side of the building looked out onto First Street. His truck was parked between this building and the law office next door, Smith Squared. That was what Kenna called the back. It was actually the side of the building, but it made her feel more comfortable to walk to the building from that vantage point, as they were hidden from view.

First Street was largely day businesses—Hairy Beards, the barbershop; Lady Liberty, another law office; Bloomin' Lovely, the flower shop; and next to that, Squeaky Clean Laundromat. All on the opposite side of First Street from here. On this side was The Paper Trail, Smith Squared, Stackable Reads bookstore, Lara's Delights, and Chestnut

Grove furniture store. All of them were now closed for business, which made the street quiet.

The loud truck drove by again on the county road and Spencer hurried to the living room and glanced out the window as it went by. Colt Lowe. He was sure of it. Looking down at his watch, it was almost eleven at night. What the hell was he doing driving back and forth?

He settled back into the sofa and decided to wait. His thoughts ranged over Kenna and what Craig had done to her today, which he'd set aside. She needed to be taken care of right now. His anger with Craig would have to wait until she was better. Even as he sat here now, every time he thought of it he wanted to put a fist through a wall, or Craig's head. But, when he thought of Kenna's fear when she saw Colt, that made his stomach roll.

He stood and paced the room, which didn't take long. It was a pleasant apartment but small and he'd easily gotten used to the large open space at the HOG. Funny how easy it was to get used to something.

He went to the kitchen and checked Kenna's refrigerator to find something to fill his rumbling tummy. Discovering diet frozen dinners in her freezer, he thought that would have to suffice for the time being. He put one in the microwave and stood by it to turn it off before it beeped. He sent Tate a message to inform him of what had gone down and decided to head to his truck to grab his laptop. He could at least get some work done.

After he'd eaten his diet meal, which, good grief, was awful—he'd tell Helissa how much he appreciated her tomorrow—he eased himself down the stairs to his truck. As he closed the door and returned to the building, the truck drove by again on the county road. This time, it cruised by far too slowly. His skin crawled that Colt was scoping out Kenna's place, and he was likely assuming they were hooking up. Which was none of his business, anyway. Still, it irritated him.

Once upstairs, he locked the door and sat at the kitchen table to get some reports written and check his emails. He also emailed his team to update them on what happened with Kenna and Craig and that he was staying here. He ended his email with a statement that he'd find out more from Kenna tomorrow before they said anything to Gerard or Jasiah. It would do no good to get things rolling up there without the full story.

He heard Kenna move in the bedroom and froze. He heard her feet pad down the hall. She stopped in the doorway to the kitchen and stared at him.

"Why are you still here?"

His heartbeat increased. She looked sleepy and sore. "I'm still taking care of you."

"It looks like you're working."

He shrugged his shoulders and grinned. "I am. I found myself hungry and wide awake, so I went down and got my laptop. I'm sorry if I woke you."

"You didn't. I keep hearing that truck go back and forth."

He swallowed and nodded. "Yeah. Me too."

She shuffled into the room and sat at the table. She looked tired, but she was likely too sore to sleep. Ibuprofen only did so much for stuff like this. "Are you hungry?"

"Yeah. I think the ibuprofen is doing a number on my tummy. It feels acidic right now."

He stood and pulled some eggs from the refrigerator. He turned on a light over the sink, so it wasn't too bright. Then he remembered Addy saying they should monitor her for light sensitivity. "Do you mind if I turn the light on?"

She slowly shook her head, and he flipped the switch. She squinted for a few moments, then she focused on him.

"Are you okay?" he asked her tentatively.

Despite her bottom lip being swollen, she smiled, sort of. "Yeah."

He opened and closed cupboards to find a plate, the pan to fry the eggs in, and silverware. He set about cracking the eggs into a bowl and whisking them together with a fork. She never said a word the entire time.

Finally, he heated the pan and poured the eggs into the melted butter.

"Do you cook a lot?"

He laughed then. He turned to face her, and she stared at him with her mouth open. "No. We have Helissa at the HOG. Growing up, we lived away from the GHOST compound, but we usually went there for meals. My mom liked to cook, but she wasn't that good at it and Mrs. James is good at it."

Kenna tilted her head to the side slightly and slowly said, "I don't understand any of what you just said."

His brows furrowed, and he swallowed. "You mean you can't hear me or it sounds garbled?"

"HOG? GHOST Compound? Helissa? Mrs. James? It sounds like a spy movie or something."

He stirred the eggs in the frying pan, and his cheeks warmed. Scooping the scrambled eggs onto a plate, he set it in front of her and pulled a fork from the drawer for her to eat with. He heated water and dropped in a tea bag, then set that in front of her before sitting in his chair.

Closing the lid on his computer, he watched her pick at her food. Her hands shook slightly.

"I guess it sounds like a spy movie. My upbringing differed from most kids. My dad is a special operative for a firm called GHOST. We handle sensitive matters the police and military usually can't do. He's my idol and my hero. Growing up around the other GHOST kids, we all played special operative games rather than kickball or volleyball. Though we played that too. But we played spy games, I guess. My teammates here now, and Aidyn, who recently left to go back home with Elena Dorsey, from Hickory Hills, went into the service and now we all work for GHOST. That's why we're here. We're trying to keep the peace between the BRR and townsfolk and support the build of the base. It's different work than what we normally do, but it's good work. Since our parents had hours that aren't the typical, we always had housekeepers and cooks to keep things going at home while we're away. And usually, we've all lived together or with other people, so community living, as it is, is normal for us."

She sat back and studied his face, which gave him time to study hers. Bruises and swelling would diminish and she would be beautiful again. And there was a quiet reserve in her he found intriguing.

"I wouldn't know what to do with people around all the time."

He chuckled. "It can get annoying when you're trying to relax, but it's also nice because I'm never bored."

The loud pipes of the truck slowly driving by caught his attention again and Kenna looked toward the window. "Who keeps driving past?"

14

She swallowed when Spencer's eyes narrowed at the window. He walked to the edge of the living room and watched the truck slowly pass. He turned toward her and didn't say a word as he sat across the table from her once again.

She finished the last of her eggs and waited until she couldn't stand it anymore. "Who is that driving by Spencer?"

His jaw muscle twitched and then shoulders tensed. She sat back and felt the tension crawl through her body. "Spencer?"

His eyes landed on hers and she saw his Adam's apple bob as he swallowed. "It's Colt Lowe."

The chills ran down her back, and she held her breath. Her fingers began shaking. She tucked her hair behind her ears and looked at her lap.

"What happened between you two, Kenna?"

She let out a shaky breath and looked toward the living room to focus on anything but his handsome face. And his beautiful eyes. She felt dirty, and not worthy, and here she was once again, beaten and battered and bruised, despite her promises to herself to never be in this position again. Even though this differed from before, there was something wrong with her. She kept ending up like this.

He stood, and she lifted her head to see him kneel in front of her. He gathered her hands up between his and held them reassuringly. "Kenna? Can you please tell me?"

She swallowed and looked deeply into his eyes. Hers watered, and he wavered before her. She blinked and felt the tears roll down her cheeks.

"We dated in high school. He was a big jock. I was a cheerleader. We were popular in school. Everyone knew Kenna and Colt." She swallowed and took in a slow, deep breath so she didn't send a riot of pain down her side. "Our senior year, I started talking about college and he got violent."

Spencer's fingers squeezed hers gently. He reached up and tucked her hair behind her right ear, then resumed holding her hands. "He beat me. At first, just a punch in the stomach. Then he'd slap me in the face. One time I had broken ribs from him kicking me. The night before I left for Houston, he beat me nearly as bad as I am right now. I packed up with my mom's help and left."

"So he's the reason you left town?"

She only nodded. What else could she say? It was true.

"Your parents didn't do anything about it?"

She shook her head. "Daddy's business would suffer. Colt was the star football player."

"He's your father!" His voice rose, but not enough to scare her.

"Small town. Business is hard to build. It's their only livelihood."

"You're their daughter."

She dragged her hands away and he let them go. He heard the pipes from the truck driving past once again and this time, he stood up fully in the living room window, where the light from the kitchen illuminated him. Just as the truck was in front of her place, she heard him step on the gas and take off. He'd likely seen Spencer was here, and he'd likely be livid, and she shuddered. She'd had plenty of nightmares about Colt Lowe coming to find her. She'd threatened her parents to never tell a soul where she lived, and it was three years before she finally told her friends where she went. Houston was a big city. It wouldn't be easy to find her there. But she still looked over her shoulder repeatedly to make sure he wasn't following her.

Spencer turned slowly and quietly came into the kitchen and picked up her plate and fork and rinsed them in the sink, then set them into the dishwasher. He did the same with the frying pan on the stove and closed the dishwasher door.

He looked at her and softly asked, "Do you need help to get back to bed?"

"No." She scooted herself to the edge of the chair and used the table for leverage to stand. She shuffled toward the bedroom, then stopped and turned to look at him. "Do you think it'll be okay if I take a bath? It might help ease some of my pain."

"I think it would be alright. I'll help you re-bandage your cuts when you get out." He moved past her and went into the bathroom and pulled the stopper on the tub and started running the water. She watched him a moment, then turned and gathered her comfy sweatpants and t-shirt and socks.

He turned the water off and slipped past her. "It's

weird for me to help you further, but if you find you need something, please let me know. I'll be a gentleman."

She smiled at him, sort of, and whispered, "I'm sure you would be."

He left her in the bathroom and closed the door, and she let the tears fall. She couldn't tell if he was mad at her or if he felt sorry for her or what his mood was, but it changed a moment ago and it set her on edge like she'd been years ago when Colt first hit her. Never sure of his mood or what would set him off, she'd always felt like she was walking on eggshells. She hated feeling like that.

She struggled with her t-shirt but got it off. She gently pulled at her bandages and gritted her teeth instead of making a sound when they pulled on her tender skin. Dropping all the soiled bandages into the wastebasket, she finally sat on the edge of the tub and lowered herself into the warm water. Laying back in the water's warmth, she let the heat seep into her body, into her bones and she let the tension slowly slide away. Tears streamed down her face and she let them mingle with the warm bath water, determined they'd be the last tears she shed over any of this bullshit. Colt Lowe could go to hell. Craig Howard could join him. And Craig's cronies up there, who helped him beat her, could make the path for them both. She was sick of being a punching bag. She was sick of being sore, and she was damned well taking her life back. Right after she healed this time.

15

Spencer finished typing up his reports, then began reading the reports his teammates had logged recently. Tate had a meeting scheduled already with Gerard and Jasiah Weston regarding bringing the electricity up the mountain. He commented on Tate's report: "Can we withhold improvements if violence is committed against any townsperson? Kenna is a mess and was simply doing her job."

He was going to probably talk to Tate about it in person, though Tate would read his comment and follow up. That's how he operated.

He heard Kenna open the bathroom door. Stepping into the hall, he saw her walk to the bedroom. "Hey, can I help you replace your bandages?"

She turned and smiled. "I would appreciate that." Holding her hand up, he saw she had all the medical supplies he needed. "I'm feeling tired and was going to manage myself after I climbed into bed. But if you're game for it, I wouldn't mind the help."

He followed her into the bedroom and held his hand

out to her as she slowly lowered herself onto the bed. She lay back and he pulled the blankets up, leaving her arms exposed for now. Sitting on the edge of the bed, he took her right hand and looked at the abrasions on her arm. There was only one that looked like it needed attention, so he set about applying the ointment and then covered it with a bandage.

Her left arm looked pretty good. The light scrapes weren't bleeding, and he left those alone for now. He lifted her blankets, and she tucked her arms under the covers. Scooting up, he looked at her face. Her eyes had cleared somewhat and weren't red. The rest had probably helped with that. With his forefinger, he gently slid the hair from her forehead to expose the gash above her right eye. His finger traced along the edge of her face as he stared at her. He swallowed, knowing he was likely taking a liberty, but he wanted to touch her. He looked into Kenna's eyes as she met his gaze. His lips hitched up at the corners and he reached for the antibiotic ointment and dabbed it on a swab, then applied it liberally but gently to the cut above her eye.

She never looked away. He could feel her eyes on him. Swallowing, he carefully laid the bandage over the ointment.

His eyes dropped to the cut on her lip. Inhaling a deep breath, he reached for a new swab, dabbed ointment on it and softly touched it to the cut on her lip. When he finished, he slowly gathered the discarded bandage wrappers and swabs.

"I wasn't sure if you were mad at me or not," she whispered.

He froze, his brows bunched together. "Why would I be mad at you?"

Her throat moved with her swallow. "Your mood changed out there."

He chuckled lightly. "Frustration. I don't understand your parents not protecting you. I don't understand why Colt would ever hit you. Hitting a woman is never acceptable. Well, unless she's attacking me. In my business, there are always exceptions. But never someone you care about. Never someone..." His voice grew quiet. "Like you."

He stood and picked up the cold teacup on her bedside table. "I'll bring you fresh tea when you wake. Sleep tight, Kenna."

"Night," she whispered.

He ambled to the kitchen, discarded the wrappers and swabs and rinsed Kenna's teacup. He pulled two bottles of water from the refrigerator and set them on the counter while he warmed fresh water for Kenna's tea.

He poured two more ibuprofen tablets from the bottle in the bathroom and found a plate in the kitchen. He laid a napkin on the plate, topped it with the ibuprofen, then set the hot cup of water on the plate. Dropping a tea bag into the cup, he picked it up, along with one bottle of water, and carried it to Kenna's bedroom.

Her deep, steady breathing made him smile. She needed the rest to heal. He left the plate next to her bed in case she woke and the bottle of water next to it should she prefer water. Exiting the bedroom, he stretched as he walked to the sofa and once again heard Colt nearing the building from the county road. He pulled his phone up and opened the video recorder and videoed Colt driving past. "It's now twelve forty-two a.m." he said while the camera was rolling.

Emailing the video to his teammates, he settled onto the sofa, hoping to get a few minutes of sleep. A couple of hours would be better, maybe even four of them. But time would tell.

His phone vibrated, and he pulled it off the coffee table to see a text from Addy.

"He's been driving close to the base as well."

Addy followed it with a clip from the video surveillance he'd set up. Colt pulled into the lot, looked at Kenna's Jeep, then sped from the lot.

"He's beat her in the past. Old boyfriend. Clearly still has issues. He's driven past here over eight times already tonight."

Henry replied.

"He's a powder keg. Watch your back."

Spencer took a deep breath and wondered just how Colt would behave in the morning on site. It would be interesting for certain. But he had nothing to be ashamed of. While he'd love to kiss Kenna, he'd kept himself the perfect gentleman. She needed help, and he was there to assist. He knew she hadn't called her parents, and he knew she wouldn't, so he was happy to be here helping her out. Otherwise, who knows what that asshole Colt would do if she were here alone?

He glanced around the room, the moonlight offering enough light that he could see some vantage points. Tomorrow he'd wire Kenna's place with cameras should Colt decide to be a jerk and do something here. They'd be able to get to Kenna without her having to call in the police.

He heard Kenna moving around again in the bedroom and got up to see if she was alright. He tapped his knuckle on the door and she said, "Come in."

"Are you alright?"

"I'm freezing again."

Spencer silently walked to the opposite side of her bed, laid his phone on the bedside table, and slid under the covers and behind her. He wrapped his arms around her body and pulled her back to his front to warm her. He fell asleep almost instantly.

16

Katrina woke, flinging her arms out from under the covers, she remembered Spencer had slid into bed to warm her up last night. She didn't protest, because it was such a sweet thing to do. But also because she liked it. With Colt driving by, she felt vulnerable again. With Spencer here with her, she felt safe. He made her feel safe.

But now? Now she was hot. And her head hurt. At least her head above her right eye hurt. It throbbed, and she wondered how long before it stopped doing that. She looked at the bedside table and saw the plate he left there with her now cold cup of tea, a bottle of water and two ibuprofen tablets. She smiled and felt the pull on her bottom lip, but she smiled just the same.

Spencer moved behind her and she turned her head to see him sitting up, with his feet flung over to the floor and scraping his hands through his hair. He had magnificent hair. It was dark, like hers, but short. It shone where the sun highlighted it. Short on the sides and back, but longer on top, the style fit him.

He glanced back at her. "Morning."

"Morning."

He stood and moved to her side of the bed. "Did you sleep well?"

"I did, finally. I don't know why the shivers keep washing over me."

"Adrenaline dump. You were crashing. The adrenaline dumped into your system to get you through the trauma, and once it leaves, your body is depleted, and the chills start."

"Thank you for keeping me warm."

His cheeks blushed pink. With his dark hair and green eyes, that hint of pink complemented his coloring perfectly.

"You're welcome. I think I fell asleep fast. Sorry. Your bed is more comfortable than sleeping on the sofa."

Her lips straightened and turned down. "I'm sorry. That isn't a very comfortable sofa."

She pushed the covers back more and turned on her side, then lifted her upper body off the mattress with both hands. She felt the pain in her ribs, but it didn't feel as bad as it did yesterday.

"Do you need help?" Spencer looked concerned and unsure of what he should be doing.

She smiled, despite the pull on her bottom lip. It didn't feel as swollen as it was yesterday. "I can manage. Thank you."

Scooting to the edge of the bed, she stood and felt rather proud of herself for managing it.

She looked up at him. "I need to use the bathroom unless you need to go first."

He shook his head. "No, I can wait. Go ahead."

Closing and locking the bathroom door, she used the

toilet and examined her knees. They had bruises on them, as well as her left thigh, but it could have been worse. Her knees were still sore from falling on them, but better than yesterday.

Washing her hands, she looked in the mirror; her eyes were clearer than yesterday too.

She pulled her hairbrush from the top drawer of her vanity and brushed her hair. Feeling as presentable as she could, she left the bathroom so Spencer could use it.

She found him in the kitchen. He stared at the coffee maker a moment, then pushed the on button and nodded. She giggled.

He whirled around and his eyes landed on hers. "I'm sorry. It was cute watching you try to figure out the coffeepot."

His brows rose into the lock of hair that fell onto his forehead. "Cute?"

She shrugged. "Yeah. There's nothing wrong with that."

She stood, watching the emotions play over his face and not for the first time she thought he was incredibly handsome. He was taller than she'd realized before, though she'd always had heels on before. Now, as she stood across the room from him, she could see how tall he was. Broad shoulders stretched his t-shirt and the muscles in his arms moved and bunched as he reached for coffee cups in the cupboard.

She swallowed as he turned, and she licked her lips to moisten them. Her tongue stopped at the cut on her bottom lip and she quickly sucked it inside her mouth as she noticed his gaze on it.

"Sit down, I'll bring your coffee. How do you like it?"

"Creamer please."

He nodded; she shuffled to the chair closest to her and lowered herself into it.

She opened her phone to read the emails she'd received and realized she had work to do. Though she wouldn't be serving any papers today. But she could sit at the computer and pull together her affidavits. Maybe she could find someone to go out to her parents' house and pick up her father's notebook.

Spencer set her coffee cup in front of her and sat across the table from her.

"Do you have to work today?" she inquired.

"Yes. Though I don't punch a clock. My duties at the base have slowed right now until the construction crew gets the walls up on the next building."

"Oh. What do you do then?"

"I'll work with the security company to install cameras and alarms. I take care of the outside for our purposes. They take care of the main security for the US military, but we're working together on it because we can share wiring and harnesses and pathways."

He took a sip of his coffee, and her eyes landed on his fingers. He had strong fingers, and she remembered him brushing her hair from her forehead last night. A thrill ran through her body at the memory. Then again, when he'd wrapped his arms around her to keep her warm. As she looked at his powerful arms now, she wondered how he could also be so gentle.

"Kenna?"

Her eyes snapped to his. He'd asked her a question. "I'm sorry." Her cheeks felt warm, and she tucked her hair behind her ear.

"Why did you go up the mountain alone yesterday?" he questioned.

"I had another set of papers to serve on Craig and Kent Bennit. I changed into jeans and a t-shirt and tennis shoes, thinking that I'd try a different tactic. I went up the other road, the one closest to here thinking maybe there'd be different men guarding it."

"Okay."

She swallowed and let out a breath. "There were different men, and I simply said I had papers for Craig to see." She sniffed lightly. "They took me to him. I could take my Jeep. I didn't have to go far. He was nearby."

Sipping her coffee to wet her throat, she finished. "I asked him his name, and he just glared at me. So I asked him if his name was Craig Howard. He said, "What's it to ya?" And I handed him the papers. He threw them back at me and told me to take my fucking papers off his mountain. I started walking to my Jeep when one of his men punched me in the side of my face." She touched the right side of her face, where she knew she was a weird shade of purple this morning. "I fell to the ground. I was so blind-sided. Another of his men came over and kicked me," she laid her right hand over her ribs on the left side, "before I could get up. When I got to my feet again, the men each took another shot at hitting me. I got to my Jeep and locked the doors. I turned around, but before I left the mountain, I rolled down my window and yelled, 'You've been served, asshole.' They had me blocked in, but I found another road across the mountain which brought me to the road near the construction site. I started crying when I saw it and I hoped you'd be there."

She squirmed in her chair as his face grew hard. Spencer laughing was glorious. Spencer mad was a whole different person. She swallowed and her fingers began shaking as she watched him. She'd never gotten over feeling afraid when Colt's moods changed. Now she realized it was anyone's mood change that scared her.

She clasped her hands together in her lap as she prepared to run if he came near her. She watched his face and his eyes captured hers and he stared. "I would have gone with you. I should have been there with you."

Her eyes rounded as she listened to him, and he cocked his head to the right.

"You're surprised to hear me say that?"

"I... um..." She let her breath out in a whoosh. "I still get nervous with major mood changes." Her cheeks burned at the admission. Boy, she was a keeper! Scared of someone's changing moods, didn't listen when he asked her to call him when she was going up there, and now she'd caused him to stay here with her as her nursemaid.

Colt's truck drove past again, and Spencer looked at his watch. "On his way to work this time."

17

Stephen stood and refilled their coffee cups. "Do you have to work tomorrow?"

"Yes. I have to draft my Affidavits of Service, but I can email them to the attorneys. But I won't be serving papers for a while. Not looking like this."

He turned after replacing the coffeepot on its burner. "So, I'd like to bring you back to the HOG. Helissa will have a nice breakfast made and Addy can look at your injuries again this morning. I can catch up with my teammates and see what's happening today, then we can go back and get your Jeep."

She stared at him for a long time. "That's a lot."

"Sorry. I know it is, but you have little to eat here, Kenna. I'm hungry and I need a shower. You need someone better than me with bandages and food. I can get you groceries for up here. I'd also like to install a security camera system here."

"Why?"

His jaw clenched. "Colt." He raised his brows as she assessed his words.

She nodded slightly. "I've been wondering what he'll do. I'm scared of him. I heard he was engaged, so I hoped he'd leave me alone, but if last night was an indicator, he'll escalate."

"Addy and Henry said he was going back and forth between the construction site and looking at your Jeep to driving past here. Clearly he was brewing on something."

She laid her hand over her stomach and her head began throbbing. Both her injury and a headache. She wasn't strong enough for this again.

Spencer moved a chair to face her and sat close. He took her hands in his and looked into her eyes. "If you think he's a danger, we'll do more than a security system. You can stay at the HOG, we have room. Or, we can figure something else out. You could stay at your parents."

"No," she snapped.

His brows rose again, this time he waited her out.

"My dad...my dad is sick. To be honest, I haven't let myself think too much about it, but I don't think he's going to make it. His heart isn't functioning as it should, and I don't even think he's telling me everything."

"Okay. So, staying with your parents is out. Do you think it's safe to stay here?"

She closed her eyes and sat back in the chair. He watched her face and saw her lip quiver slightly.

"I don't know. I've spent the past ten years worried about Colt. After I left here, I looked over my shoulder every damned day, afraid he'd come after me. He threatened all the time we were together that if I ever left, he'd search until he found me. That fear—it consumed me day and night. After a few years, I relaxed. I'd ask my mom if Colt was still in town, and he caused so much trouble that she always knew he was around. So, I relaxed more. But, I always look over my shoulder and I'm always just on the edge of running. So, to answer your question, now that I'm here and he's still here and his behavior last night... What do you think?"

"That you'll stay at the HOG."

"I don't want to do that. I don't know anyone out there but you and Addy. And I don't really know either of you."

She twisted her fingers in her lap and his heart felt heavy that he'd made her nervous. He held his hands open in front of her and she put her nervous hands in his. He closed his fingers around hers and looked into her eyes. "I didn't mean to make you nervous. I'm trying to figure out what we can do to keep you safe. The HOG is safe. But I can wire this place with cameras and security and if he tried to get in here, we'd know in an instant and be here in no time."

She bit the opposite side of her bottom lip from the cut and he watched her eyes dart around and finally land on his. "Do you think you could stay here? Just one more night. You can sleep in the bed with me...if it's not too weird. It's more comfortable. I'll be quiet and I can get some groceries and cook for you. I'm not bad. Maybe not as good as Helissa or Mrs. James, but I'll try."

He smiled at her, and her breath caught. "I think we can make that work. If it doesn't, promise me you'll think about staying out at the HOG."

"I promise."

She leaned forward and kissed his lips. It was brief. Too brief. She pulled back and smiled slightly. "I've been thinking about that for a while now. I'm sorry."

He chuckled. "Don't be sorry. It was nice."

"It was?"

"It was." He leaned in and gently kissed her lips. A little longer this time. But soft so as not to hurt her lip.

When he pulled back, her cheeks had turned a rosy pink.

She swallowed. "That was nice."

He grinned. "It was."

He scooted his chair back. Nothing else could happen right now. She was in no shape, and he didn't want to think of taking advantage of her. She was battered, scared, and relieved a bit that she wouldn't be alone while Colt was out there driving around and stalking her. That's likely all that was; a thank you kiss.

But he thought she was brave, maybe too stubborn. But lonely and maybe sad and something about her called to him in a way he'd never known before. She was quiet with reserve and strength and beauty. Lord, was she beautiful! And she was so strong. It appeared she had to be, but he wanted to be strong with her, so she wasn't so alone. No one should have to shoulder the burdens of the world alone, and certainly not when you've been beaten down. So, he'd be her strength for a while and maybe, just maybe they'd steal a few kisses here and there and get to know each other a little better. Maybe.

18

Kenna stood in the kitchen at the HOG, staring at what they'd done with this place. It used to be an old sewing factory back in the day. But, this. Wow! They'd done an amazing job with the remodel. They exposed the original brick and sealed it in a matte sealer. The wooden cabinets stood out nicely against the brick. The granite counters were shiny and beautiful. The room was airy and bright, yet still cozy.

Helissa didn't look up, nodded her head and smiled. "You eat while Spencer cleans up. Then I'll pack you a lunch and maybe something for dinner, so you're all set."

"Thank you so much. You don't have to do that."

Helissa waved a hand in her direction and kept on cooking. Addy entered the room. "Good morning, Kenna. How are you today?"

"I'm fine. How are you?"

Addy chuckled. "I'm great. I see you've met Helissa, and she's already trying to fatten you up."

Addy smiled at Helissa, which prompted Helissa to respond, "You're too thin. You need to fatten up."

Addy sat at the counter next to her and pointed to her plate. "Finish your breakfast."

"What about you?"

Addy chuckled. "I ate about an hour ago."

Kenna nibbled at her food, unable to open her mouth without splitting her wound open.

Spencer entered the room, saw her eating, and nodded. "That's good. Get some nutrition in you." He looked at Addy. "Morning, Addy. What's happening today?"

She shrugged. "I'm waiting for Tate. He's meeting with Gerard and Jasiah today and I don't know if he wants me there to discuss Kenna's injuries."

Kenna turned to Addy. "Why?"

Spencer took a plate from Helissa and sat on the other side of her as Addy answered. "Because Gerard is the vice president of the BRR and Jasiah, his son, is the secretary. Tate has been brokering peace with them without Craig, because he's unreasonable. But they need to know that him assaulting you, or any citizen, will be held against them when it comes to bringing utilities up the mountain."

"Oh."

Spencer swallowed and asked, "Did you serve Kent yesterday?"

"No. I didn't see him. I still have to do that."

"That you can do down here. We'll ask Gerard and Jasiah to bring Kent down here for the papers. They'll be with him and he won't cause trouble. Honestly, he's been taking part in the peace talks with us. But it doesn't excuse his behavior prior to that."

"No, it doesn't," she responded. Scooping another bite of egg onto her fork, she put it in her mouth.

Helissa pulled out some containers. "Spencer, will you be with Kenna today? I'm packing food."

"Yes. I'll be staying at her place for at least tonight."

Helissa nodded, and Kenna wondered what everyone thought of that. Spencer staying at her place for two nights in a row. It looked like things were different than they were. But part of her, a sassy part of her, didn't want to explain it. He was an incredible man. Handsome, strong, tall, broad, muscly and kind. She could do worse.

Another man walked into the kitchen. "Morning."

He held his hand out to her. "I'm Tate Vickers. You must be Kenna."

"Yes. Hi. Kenna Lawrence," she responded around a mouthful of food.

Tate nodded and poured himself a cup of coffee. When he turned, he said, "I understand you're going out with the girls tonight."

Her body became rigid. She'd forgotten. Staring into his eyes, she swallowed. "I forgot." She laid her fork on her plate and folded her hands together on her lap. "I can't...like this. I don't want to be seen..."

Spencer reached under the counter and held her hands. Both of her hands fit in his grasp. Her mind wandered as she thought about this. But her mind caught the last of his words. "...at your place or here."

Addy shrugged. "I'm fine with either. We'll just sit and chitchat. At your place, we can talk about men and how evil they are without the men being around."

"You don't do that—do you?" Kenna asked.

Addy laughed. "No. Not really. We work with some great men here and we don't have the horrible experiences that many women do. But you and Lara may have some things to say about the subject."

Tate's brows rose into his hairline. "Lara has no complaints where I'm concerned."

Addy laughed again. "Most men don't think so."

Spencer leaned forward and looked past her to Addy. "You're digging yourself in deep, Addy."

She shrugged. "Naw. I'm sure Tate's right."

Tate shook his head and let out a deep breath. "Spencer, what do you plan to do about Colt?"

"I'm going to install security cameras at Kenna's today. Beyond that, there isn't much we can do until he tries something. But keeping her feeling safe and catching him on camera will help us put his ass in jail if he tries anything."

She turned to Spencer. Her eyes locked on his, but she said nothing. She wasn't sure what to say, to be honest.

He grinned at her. "Are you finished with breakfast?"

Nodding, she pushed her plate back, and Helissa scoffed. "You're too skinny."

"I'm sorry. It's delicious. Really. It's just hard to eat today."

Helissa shrugged and opened the refrigerator. She opened a can of something and poured it into a glass. Setting it in front of her, Helissa nodded. "Nutritional drink. At least you'll get your vitamins."

"Thank you." She sipped at her drink as Tate and Addy chatted about her being present today at their meeting.

Spencer mentioned having Kent come with them so she could serve him, and Tate nodded. "Kenna, will you be able to stop in at the Sheriff's Department this afternoon to serve Kent?"

"Yes. Thank you."

"Don't put makeup on."

Her eyes widened. But he continued. "He needs to see what they did to you. They all do. You'll be safe. We won't let anything happen. Spencer, you come with her."

Without waiting for a response, Tate left the room, and she felt the throbbing in her head once again.

Addy whispered, "Ready for me to take a look?"

19

She watched him running a wire through the wall of her office anyway. He'd wired the front cameras, the back cameras, and on all sides of the building outside. Now he was running the wires to her upstairs entry door, where he'd put another control panel.

"Why don't you run the wires outside and tuck them in a conduit or something?" she asked.

"This way, they can't be cut."

He nodded and he grinned at her. Tapping his forehead with his forefinger, he chuckled. "I have a method to my madness."

She smiled and nodded. "I can see that."

She'd brought her laptop upstairs and locked up the business doors for the day. She could receive emails and phone calls, but she didn't want to see anyone.

She called Attorney Murphy and said that she had delivered the paperwork to Craig the prior day. She worked quietly and efficiently, and he enjoyed listening to her contact clients and arrange for affidavits or other services.

He tried not making a mess but pulling wires through insulation in the walls was messy business. He'd have to vacuum when he finished. He hated vacuuming.

His phone timer went off. Kenna was seated at the kitchen table. She'd put on a pair of shorts as the afternoon heated. Though her knees were bruised where she fell yesterday, she had nice legs. Smooth skin and shapely calves. He hadn't noticed a woman's calves in, well, ever.

"We have to get ready to head to the Sheriff's Department, Kenna."

Her eyes looked up from her computer and her pretty lips formed a straight line before she closed the lid on her laptop. He brushed his hands together to remove the dust and moved toward her.

"I'll be with you the entire time."

She stood, less pained now than earlier, which was a bonus. "I know. I appreciate that."

He watched as she walked past him to her bedroom. She had a nice ass, too. Her long, dark, thick hair swung behind her and trailed down her back. She was stunning. Brunettes were his favorite. Green-eyed brunettes, well those ladies intrigued him immensely.

He turned toward the wires he'd been pulling and decided to at least hook up the control panel while she prepared to go. That was the easiest part of the installation. The hardest was setting everything up on the apps.

Kenna stepped from the bedroom, looking fresh and beautiful. Despite the bruising and swelling on her face, she was a vision. She'd changed into dress slacks that hung loosely over her legs and a yellow short-sleeved blouse that mingled with her coloring perfectly.

He stared a bit too long, and she fidgeted. "Is this..."

"You look stunning."

"I'm sure." Her hand touched the right side of her face.

"You do. You have the prettiest eyes I've ever seen."

Her cheeks turned pink, and that added more to her already-gorgeous appearance.

She nodded and heaved out a deep breath.

Holding his hands up, he shook his head. "Just let me wash my hands."

He turned to the sink and squirted soap from the dispenser and washed the dust and insulation off his hands and arms before approaching her.

She tipped her head up to look into his eyes. He licked his lips and softly touched them to hers. He held his lips to hers for a few moments, then pulled away. Her arms wrapped around his waist and she laid her head against his chest. Gently, he wrapped his arms around her and they stood together, steady, solid, for a few moments.

His pulse quickened and the sensations that surged through his body were unlike any he'd ever experienced. He inhaled sharply. His hands smoothed over her back, adding pressure enough to let her know he enjoyed having her against him like this.

She loosened her arms first, but he quickly followed her lead. He swallowed, "Ready?"

"Yeah."

He turned to the side so she could step past him, but he kept his hand at the small of her back. As he opened his truck door, he held his hand out to help her up into the seat. He grinned at her as he buckled her in.

"I can fasten my seatbelt," she said with a chuckle.

"I know, but I kind of like it."

Her cheeks turned a soft pink, and he winked at her before closing the door and striding around the front of the truck to his side.

During the short ride to the sheriff's department Kenna twisted her hands in her lap, on top of the folder that held Kent's papers. He reached over and squeezed her hands. "I'll be right there with you. Every step of the way."

She nodded. "I appreciate it."

He pulled into the parking lot and saw Tate's truck already there. He pointed it out to Kenna, and she nodded.

He helped her from the truck and walked with his hand on the small of her back. Inside, the receptionist smiled as she looked up, then her eyes widened when she saw Kenna's face.

"If you follow me, the sheriff is expecting you," she blurted.

Down the hallway, he kept contact with her as they strode into the conference room where the sheriff, Tate, and Addy sat talking, all eyes turned to them.

Sheriff Cranford's lips turned down into a frown when he saw Kenna. Spencer didn't want her feeling any more self-conscious than she already did, so he quickly nodded to the sheriff and held his hand out to shake. Sheriff Cranford shook his hand, then quietly offered Kenna a seat at the table next to Addy. He took the chair on the other side of her.

"Can I get you something to drink, Kenna?" the sheriff offered.

"No, thank you."

She put the papers for Kent on top of the table and folded her hands over them. Within a minute, the receptionist buzzed the sheriff. "Sheriff, Gerard and Jasiah Weston are here with Kent Bennit."

The sheriff glanced at Kenna, and she nodded.

Spencer's heart swelled with pride for this tiny woman. She'd been through hell, but she was here, sitting before the people who represented those who had harmed her, and she did it gracefully.

The door opened, and he noticed the slight jump she made. He turned to look into her eyes and she frowned slightly, but nodded.

The three men entered the room and shook hands with all the others. Kenna stood and looked each of them in the eye as she extended her hand in greeting.

They were stone silent as the sheriff began explaining her presence. Gerard glanced at Kent, who then hung his head before saying, "I'm so sorry I wasn't there to help you."

Gerard asked, "Where were you?"

"I was down here looking for a job. I had an interview at Cyber Secure, for networking support," Kent replied.

Gerard nodded, then glanced at Kenna once again. "He'll take the papers you have for him, Ms. Lawrence."

Kenna nodded and opened the manila folder in front of her. She held the papers up and looked at Kent. "Are you Kent Bennit?"

"Yes ma'am. I am."

She held the papers out to him, a slight shake to them. "You have been served a Summons and Complaint."

Kent took the papers gently from her hands. "Yes, ma'am." Kent nodded and held the papers in front of him but didn't read them.

Kenna sat once again and glanced at her watch while Tate explained their stance on Craig's behavior and how he couldn't behave like this. He'd recommend to the town council that they withhold utilities from the mountain as long as citizens were not safe going up there. Kenna was doing her job. Any workers going up there to install utilities would do their jobs and the BRR would guarantee safety before making any improvements.

Addy recounted Kenna's injuries, and the men all stared at her face, usually incredibly beautiful, now a dark shade of purple marred by cuts and abrasions.

Once Addy finished, Kenna turned to him. "May we leave now?" she whispered.

He leaned over and looked at Tate. "Do you need us, Tate?"

Tate shook his head. "No. Thank you both for coming in."

Without another word, Kenna stood and they walked out of the room, his hand once again at the small of her back.

Outside, the sun glowed in the sky and Kenna tilted her head back and closed her eyes as the sun warmed her skin. He did the same thing. "This feels good."

"It does," she agreed.

20

As sunlight still warmed their faces, Kenna reached over and took Spencer's hand in hers. His gaze fell on her and he smiled.

She chuckled. "Are you finally ready to go home?"

"That I am. How about you?"

"Yeah. I'm ready. I can now let Ms. Smith know I've effected service on all parties."

He nodded. "I'm proud of you. You're badass."

She chuckled. "Hardly."

"Kenna, honey, your hands barely shook as you handed Kent those papers. You faced them, let them see your condition, and you didn't flinch. Badass."

"We have different ideas of what badass means."

He escorted her to the truck and helped her in. This time when he reached over to buckle her seat belt, she put her hand on his shoulder. When he looked up into her eyes, she leaned in and kissed his lips lightly.

"Thank you, Spencer."

"For what?"

"For taking care of me. For making me feel safe. For

calling me badass." Her smile was genuine. His heart thumped along happily.

He leaned forward and kissed her. She wanted to kiss him so much more, but he pulled away. He winked. "You are badass, and I love it."

She giggled, and he strutted around the truck, feeling like a man with a great secret.

He pulled out of the sheriff's department parking lot and drove toward the construction site to pick up her Jeep.

As he drove, he reached over and took her hand. She was twenty-eight years old, and she felt giddy holding hands with a boy. But he was so much more than a boy. He was a handsome man, and he made her feel safe and cared for like no one ever had in her life.

They pulled into the parking lot at the construction site, and he parked next to her Jeep. She waited for him to walk around and help her out. She'd never had a man do this for her in her entire life. In movies, she'd seen the women wait for the men to help them and she enjoyed the chivalry and manners. Many southern men still did this for their women. Her dad had always been gentlemanly with her mom. But when she dated Colt all those years ago, he never held her door or helped her in or out of the car. At first she'd been a bit taken aback by that and told him a gentleman always opened doors for women or helped them in and out of the car as a sign of good manners. He'd told her to get off her high horse and be the modern woman she wanted to be. So she did that, but her heart longed for a gentleman.

Spencer made her enjoy this. First, she enjoyed watching him when he walked in front of the truck. She seemed to find something new to admire about him every time she studied him. His hair was short but very dark.

Today she noticed how at just two in the afternoon he already had a rugged-looking five-o'clock shadow beginning on his face.

His t-shirt stretched across the muscles of his chest as he reached for the door handle. She could see the defined pecs as the sun brightened the color of his gray t-shirt. She couldn't see his abs, but she'd felt them when she hugged him this morning. He'd been solid and firm against her, and she hadn't felt so safe her entire life. Especially since Colt. She hadn't felt safe since him—ever. Until now.

She turned herself in the seat and held his hand as she stepped on the running board of his truck, then stepped to the ground. She'd worn tennis shoes today because her legs were still sore from falling yesterday and she didn't want to make them worse by wearing heels. Sure-footedness it would be for a few days.

He opened her Jeep door, then his brows bunched. "Are you feeling strong enough to shift? You could drive my truck and I can take your Jeep if you prefer."

"I think I should be alright. I'm a little sore, but I think it's manageable."

"Okay. It's not far, but if you change your mind, just pull over and we'll trade."

"Thank you." Her cheeks felt a rush of heat. She was getting used to that with Spencer. She blushed at the way he looked at her and the way he treated her. Sometimes she had to shake her head. She was getting so turned around by him.

She used the steering wheel to heft herself up into the Jeep. She froze as she sat, a lightning bolt of pain shooting down her side where she'd been kicked in the ribs.

"Are you alright?"

At the sound of his husky voice, she blinked rapidly as tears filled her eyes. "Yeah. I just..." She cleared her throat. "I forgot about my ribs being so sore. Stupid, really."

He looked into her eyes, and the hushed timbre of his voice sent a whole different bolt of lightning through her body. "Don't be so hard on yourself. It'll take time, but remember, you're badass."

Emotions so foreign to her rushed forward and back, and her brain struggled to process them. So many feelings running through her as she stared into his eyes. One side of his lips curled up into a cute grin and that—wow, that made her nipples pucker.

Footsteps approaching had Spencer turning and the instant he did, his back straightened and the muscles in his shoulders bunched. His hands fisted, and she braced herself for something, not sure what.

"Hey, are you alright?" Colt yelled.

"She's fine, Colt."

"I didn't ask you—Romeo!" Colt spat.

"Romeo? Really?"

"Kenna. I asked you a question."

"She doesn't have to answer your questions, Colt. Now, back up."

"I don't have to follow your orders, Spencer." Colt mocked.

Another voice entered the mix and Kenna tried to see who it was, but the stabbing pain in her ribs kept her from doing so. "That's enough. Colt, get back to the job or I'm going to have a chat with Baxter about your worth here. Kenna and Spencer are none of your business."

"Fuck you, Henry."

She heard Colt pivot, the gravel under his boots sliding and crunching.

Silence met her ears, and she tried looking in her rearview mirror to see what she could see. Twisting slowly in her seat so her knees faced Spencer alongside her, she could see Colt glaring at Henry and Spencer glaring at Colt, just like Henry. Colt turned back to Spencer and then took a step toward her when Spencer stepped to the side, blocking Colt from coming any closer.

"Get the fuck out of my way, Spencer," Colt barked.

Spencer answered right back. "Come one step closer and you'll look just like you've made Kenna look many times in her life."

Colt took another step closer and Spencer slowly turned to her and lifted her legs into the Jeep. "Stay in here, honey," he whispered. Then he closed her door. He pointed to the locks. "Lock it up."

She did as he asked, then she watched as if in slow motion as Colt moved in again and in one huge, hard punch, Spencer downed him.

Spencer's muscles tightened like a rope ready to snap. His jaw clenched, his back was ramrod straight and his hands were balled into fists, waiting for Colt to get up and punch him back.

Instead, Colt stood slowly, his back to her. His head was down and he held the side of his face as he walked past Henry, bumping him slightly as he moved past and then he disappeared behind Spencer's pickup truck.

She turned the key in her ignition so she could roll her window down. Spencer faced her, and she watched in amazement as his face softened.

His voice was gravelly when he spoke to her. "Are you alright?"

She swallowed. "I'm badass. Are you alright?"

He grinned. It was beautiful. Like magic dust sprinkled over him. "I'm good."

She stared into his eyes. "You're amazing. Like a..." She shook her head slightly. "Like you take my breath away."

They stared at each other for a long time. She saw his throat convulse as he swallowed repeatedly. When he spoke, it was as if he was so surprised he couldn't put the words together. "You don't even know how that makes me feel right now."

21

Sucked his lungs full of air as he ambled to his truck. He navigated through the maze of thoughts and feelings and felt perplexed about his progress. She made him feel things he'd never felt before. He was thirty-one years old, and she had his insides all knotted together so much so he didn't know where one emotion began and another one ended.

The attraction was certainly there, of course—she was gorgeous. But she was so much more than that. She was smart, so damned smart. She was professional. He'd enjoyed listening to her talk to her clients this morning, and he got a better idea of who Kenna Lawrence was as a businesswoman. She called the phone company to change over their landline and he listened as she explained how she wanted it to work. Then she negotiated a great price for the service to boot. She wasn't as prone to hysterics as many people would be. Stoic. She'd gotten the shit kicked out of her yesterday and while at first she cried, and a few more times the tears flowed yesterday, she wasn't a hysterical mess. She processed everything with such grace and poise. Dammit, he admired the shit out of her. Then today, at the sheriff's department, color him completely enamored as she faced the three men across the table from her with a quiet reserve he didn't even feel.

Hopping into his truck, he caught Kenna's eye through the windows; she smiled and gave him a thumbs-up.

He smiled, returned the signal and waited for her to back her Jeep up and head toward her place. He followed closely in case she had any trouble, but she didn't. It looked like she did just fine without his help at all. That gave him mixed feelings. He enjoyed being needed by Kenna.

Once at her place, he assisted her to the apartment door.

She stopped in the doorway. "I should check the mail."

"I'll run and get it. You go on up and I'll be right there."

He jogged to the mailbox on First Street and pulled it open. There were several letters, a magazine, and far too many fliers and postcards advertising this, that and the other. Trying to stack it in some order so he dropped nothing, he heard the loud pipes of Colt's truck. He turned just as Colt gunned the truck toward him. He dove out of the way as the mailbox flew into the air and landed a few feet from where he laid.

He scrambled to his feet and Kenna came out the door.

"Spencer!" she yelled.

He got to his feet as Colt spun around and raced toward him. He ran to Kenna and hustled her toward the building. "Get inside."

She made her way back to the front porch and Spencer turned to see Colt aim at him, then veer off at the last minute. He called to Kenna, "Get your phone out and record this bastard!"

He grabbed the mailbox laying crumpled on the ground near the Smith Squared law office. Two office girls had stepped out onto their front porch, one of them on the phone. He set the mailbox to the side to fix later. Colt's truck came barreling down the street once again and he turned to see Colt veer into the parking area of The Paper Trail, barely missing him and his truck, then shooting across the small patch of grass between The Paper Trail and Smith Squared and out of the parking lot.

Sirens sounded, and he looked down the street to see if Colt was coming back or if he also heard the sirens. No sign of Colt or his truck.

Spencer walked toward Kenna and felt instantly better when she hugged him. He held her close, though now he was feeling a few aches and pains from his deep dive onto the blacktop. A police squad car screeched to a halt in front of Smith Squared.

The officer exited her squad car and strutted toward the women on the porch at Smith Squared. She chatted a moment with the women, watched a video one of them made, then walked toward him. He glanced at Kenna, who was making her way down the front steps of the building, and waited for her to join him. He laid his arm around her shoulders.

"I'm Officer Bradley. Can you tell me what happened here?"

He held his hand out to Officer Bradley. She looked down at his hand, which was now bleeding from the scrapes on the blacktop. Her face blanched and he pulled his hand back.

Kenna said, "I'll go get the first aid kit."

"I'm alright, Kenna."

"Shush," she said as she limped away.

Officer Bradley looked him in the eye. "Before you tell me what happened here, what happened to Kenna's face?"

"Craig Howard and his goons."

She sucked in a breath. "Is she alright?"

"She's doing okay. I've been helping her out. Nothing's broken, but she's pretty sore. She took a vicious beating."

"It looks as though she did."

He nodded and tucked his hands into his front pockets. Remembering the blood, he dropped his hands down to his sides. "Colt Lowe made this mess here." He waved his arm out toward the parking area and where the mailbox used to be. Some pieces of mail still littered the parking area.

"Why did he do that?"

"I suspect it's because I punched him earlier today."

Officer Bradley looked him in the eyes.

"Why did you punch Colt Lowe?"

Kenna came out of the building and moved toward them. "See her face? Colt used to do that to her back when they dated in high school. She left town because she was afraid of him. Last night, he drove back and forth past this place eight or nine times. I recorded a few of them. Harassing Kenna."

Kenna came to stand near him, but she stopped and looked up at him. He continued, "Today, he barked out questions to Kenna when we went back to the construction site to pick up her vehicle. He scared her, and I told him to back off. He didn't. I told him again and my teammate told him as well. He didn't listen and when he got too close to Kenna, I punched him."

Officer Bradley looked at Kenna and nodded. Kenna

pulled his right hand toward her and cracked open a water bottle. She poured the water on his hand, which stung, but he didn't let on. She dabbed it dry with a gauze pad, then applied antibiotic ointment to it. They'd have to invest in antibiotic ointment at this rate.

"Did you see what happened today, Kenna?" Officer Bradley asked her.

"I did." Kenna reached for his left hand and repeated her nursing. "I saw all of it."

"Including the punch?"

"Yep."

"Was it provoked?"

"Yes ma'am. Colt is real good at provoking."

Once Kenna finished with his hands, she pulled her cell phone from her back pocket and tapped a few times. She turned her phone around and showed Officer Bradley the video she'd taken of Colt trying to run him down. Or terrorize him at the least.

Officer Bradley watched the video and asked, "Can you forward that to me?" She pulled out a business card and Kenna's fingers flew over her phone. As soon as she finished, she handed Officer Bradley her card back. "All set."

"You may want to keep my card in case you need it."

"Thank you, but it's faster to call 911. Hopefully, I won't need to. That is, if you can keep Colt from driving past my house every hour all night long, revving his pipes to wake me up and harass me. I swear his fiancée must be dim-witted to be engaged to a jackass like that."

"He's engaged?"

"Yes ma'am. To Ami Pearson."

"I'd appreciate it if you'd come back to the station to make a statement. I'll type up our conversation here and you can sign it. If you can't get there, I'll be back around to have you look at it and sign it later."

Spencer nodded at her. "Either way is fine with us, officer. Just let us know when your report is ready."

Officer Bradley walked away, and he turned to pick up the mail laying in the parking area. Kenna followed behind him, taking the envelopes as he picked them up. Then he nodded toward the apartment. "I'm ready to get out of the sun. How about you?"

Leaving wouldn't be much different. She'd left here once because of Cole, but now her father needed her and leaving wasn't an option. Yet. Once her father was better, or if the worst happened and he passed, she'd close up shop and move back to Houston. Or somewhere. She didn't have a job there now, and she didn't have a place to live either. She'd hired a moving company to transport her items back here, then she hopped on a plane to get here sooner than she'd planned because her mom had said her father wouldn't make it. That was a week ago, and this had been a long-ass week.

Kenna landed on the last step and let out a long sigh.

Spencer's voice was close behind her. "It's exhausting, isn't it?"

"Yes." She inhaled and turned to face him. "I need a nap."

His head tilted down slightly, and his lips curled up in the sexiest smile. "Go on and lay down. I want to get this security system installed."

"Don't you want to rest after what you've been through?"

"Yes, of course. But I need to make sure we're all set in case Colt causes more trouble."

She felt conflicted. Spencer had been the perfect gentleman since he'd been here. They'd kissed a few times, and she liked it. Her lip was split, so she couldn't kiss him like she wanted right now. And she doubted he'd want to have sex with her looking like a punching bag. But she wanted to feel a closeness with him. She wanted—something more.

She sucked her bottom lip softly between her teeth and swallowed. "Thank you." She stood on her toes and kissed his lips.

When she pulled back, his eyes rounded, then his brows rose into his hairline. His sensual lips slowly curved into the most beautiful smile. She sighed.

His head dipped, and she closed her eyes. The touch of his soft lips on hers beguiled her. She opened her mouth as far as she could and he accepted her invitation. His tongue slid sensually along hers, then slid back out before sliding in once again.

"I don't want to hurt you."

"Good," she whispered.

His knees bent, and his hands slid to her behind. He lifted her up against his body, and he did it without hurting her. Her arms circled his neck and her legs wrapped around his waist. Pulling back, she stared into his eyes.

He kissed her bruised temple, and around her battered eye. "Kenna," he whispered in her ear. His tongue then swiped around the shell of her ear, and a dizzying riot of feelings zinged through her body. She clenched her thighs. Spencer pulled back and locked eyes with her.

"I don't know how to do this without hurting you."

She kissed his neck, then her lips kissed a path up his jaw and to his ear where she mimicked his actions a moment ago. He huffed out a breath, and she smiled.

"Take me into the bedroom, Spencer," she murmured.

He moved slowly down the short hallway to her bedroom. His muscles bunched under her hands which sent more excitement flying through her body. He laid her gently on the bed, so careful with her, she felt like a precious glass bauble.

He laid between her legs, holding himself up on his elbows. Their lips touched and moved. She could feel his desire grow both in the passion of his kisses and where their bodies touched. He rubbed his length against her, and she grew wet and hot and excited to make love to him.

As their bodies heated, the aroma of his aftershave floated around them and she inhaled deeply. She wanted to remember how he smelled and felt.

She wanted to remember him forever. She hadn't been with another man in years. The vulnerable feelings usually made her panic and run by this point.

But now, the last thing she wanted to do was run.

Spencer's hands cupped her head as he gently kissed her face, then down her neck. He pushed her blouse up her body, careful not to brush her ribs, then his lips kissed her chest until he reached the lacy material of her bra. He pushed her bra up over her breasts and his mouth sucked her right nipple into his mouth and his tongue flicked it. She puckered so tightly the sensations ran straight to her core. She lifted her hips to push into his body, but he simply kissed across her chest to her left breast and played with her nipple. He sucked her breast firmly into his mouth and she huffed out a breath.

He began trailing kisses to the waistband of her slacks. The ringing of his phone breached their passionate sounds. He froze with his lips resting against her belly. It rang again.

"Fuck," he muttered.

"Ignore it."

"I can't. What if it's about Colt?"

She lay back against the bed, wishing she'd never hear Colt's name. Ever again.

Spencer rolled to his back next to her as his phone rang again. He pulled it from his back pocket. "Yeah." He huffed out.

She couldn't hear who was on the other end of the phone, but it was a man's voice. Spencer sat up, "When?"

He walked across her bedroom and looked out the window. "Okay."

She turned to her side and pushed herself up to a sitting position, righting her bra and her blouse. Sadly.

"Okay. Thanks for letting me know." He clipped.

He listened for a moment more and she took a deep breath, pleased that it didn't send a gut punch from her sore ribs.

As he pocketed his phone, he turned toward her. "I have to go."

"Where?"

"The construction office. The computers aren't working and the security cameras are offline."

Spencer kissed her forehead, then wrapped his big powerful arms around her body and held her close.

She liked it. Even just this. Him holding her close, his

aftershave filling her nostrils, his strength propping her up.

Kissing the top of her head, he said, "Stay here. Inside. Keep the doors locked. I'll be back as soon as I can."

"Okay."

She felt a loss as she followed him down the hallway. He touched the control panel, still hanging by the wires he'd connected to it. Picking up the drill sitting on the counter, he drilled two holes above the panel and within thirty seconds, he had it attached to the wall.

"It's not fully operational yet, but you can push this button right here when I close the door downstairs. That will set the alarm, and if anyone tries to get in, I'll get a notification on my phone. Later on, I'll get the rest of it set up and we'll get the app on your phone so you can control it from wherever you are."

"Okay."

He grinned and holy hell, that little one-sided grin made her weak in the knees. "I'll call you when I get back, so you can turn the alarm off."

"Okay."

He kissed her lips quickly, pointed to the button on the control panel, then strutted down the steps to the back door.

Just before closing the door, he glanced up at her and she nodded. Spencer closed the door behind him and she pushed the button. The light went red, the readout on the screen said, 'Armed.'

23

Stared at the clock for what seemed like the hundredth time. He let out a sigh and continued working on the security software.

"Figure it out yet?" Henry asked from behind him.

"No." He scraped his hand through his hair. "They've hacked the system. And every time I think I've got it sorted, it jams up on me." He tapped a few keys and tried another trick with the computer. He glanced at Henry. "Did you unplug the cameras and then plug them back in?"

"Yeah. But the system seems so slow. It took a while for the lights to come back up."

"Yeah." He clicked between screens and tried to reconnect the cameras once again. This time they blinked and sputtered but came up on the screen. "Finally!"

Henry looked over his shoulder and they both waited for every camera to come up before feeling good about this progress.

As the last camera connected, he reached his hand up and Henry high-fived him.

"Okay, now I'll check each camera's schedules and make sure they're focused."

Henry stepped back to the entrance door. "I'll be doing another perimeter walk just to make sure nothing's happened since the cameras were down."

"Thanks, Henry."

Spencer glanced at the clock on his computer once more. He'd been at it for five hours now. He stood as he waited for his computer to connect all the dots to each of the hardware pieces he had in place. Lifting his arms, he stretched his back muscles, feeling the ones he'd abused earlier today when he'd dodged Colt's truck. He still hadn't heard from the sheriff about whether they'd stopped Colt and arrested him for that little number.

He got a text from Maya.

"We're on our way over to Kenna's. Are you still working?"

"Yeah. I've got another couple of hours here."

"Sounds good. We'll make sure she's safe till you return."

She'd been safe all afternoon as far as he knew. She hadn't called him and nothing had triggered the app for her cameras on his phone. He remembered the security system then texted Maya once again.

"Call Kenna when you get there. I have the security system only half installed, and she'll need to push the unarmed button to let you in."

She responded with a thumbs-up.

He sat at the computer once more and started searching through the files he'd quarantined. Who the hell had hacked this system? It was sophisticated and, he'd thought, hack proof. Someone with some tricky computer knowledge had gotten inside their system.

The trailer door opened, and Tate stepped inside. "Figure it out?"

"Yeah. The cameras are up and running again and I've quarantined the files that affected them."

"Who do you think had the knowledge to do something like this?"

Spencer turned and faced his friend and boss. "I've been wondering about Kent Bennit."

Tate's brows rose into his hairline. The thoughts going through his brain played out on his face. He heaved out a deep breath. "Tell me why."

Spencer shook his head and shrugged. "I don't have any solid proof. But last year Kent hacked into police squads, security systems around town, and even the stoplights and shut things down on a whim. Today, Kenna served him with court papers because he's being sued for the damage he caused in town. It may have set him off."

Tate heaved out a heavy sigh as he sat down. "I'm not saying you're wrong, but he's been working with us for months now. He's even applying for jobs down here."

"I know. He mentioned that today. And he looked horrified to see Kenna's face. He apologized for not being there to protect her. He said he was at a job interview."

"His interview was with Cyber Secure." Tate scratched his chin.

"I'm not saying he's the one for sure. I don't have the proof. He's just the first person who came to mind."

Tate stood. "Okay. Glad you're getting things sorted in here. We'll keep this between ourselves for right now. I'll do some questioning and see if Kent is up to something. In case it isn't him, though, keep scouring the quarantined files for information."

"Will do."

Once he finished with the bug scour, he'd check schedules and make sure each camera pointed in the correct direction. Then he'd go back to Kenna's.

His thoughts hadn't left her since he'd gotten here today. They were close to having sex this afternoon. He wanted to. He wanted her. She was incredible, and he'd grown more and more fond of her as they spent time together. But she'd be leaving soon, and he'd do well not to get attached.

But having sex and enjoying each other shouldn't be out of the question. She knew she was leaving, and she was ready to have sex with him. So, it's not like she was planning a lifelong partnership here. And, when she left, they'd likely both be ready to move on. His only long-lasting relationship had been six months. They were both in the service and when he transferred to another base; they parted as friends, promised to keep in touch, but never did.

He'd always wondered about that. Once in a while he thought of calling her, but didn't because he felt like she could have called him, but she didn't. So he could have a good time here with Kenna while she was here and when she left, it would be just fine.

That thought process finished, he set about checking the cameras' schedules so he could get home to Kenna. Hopefully, she was having fun with the girls while he was out. Hopefully, she didn't decide she didn't want him around anymore after her night with the girls. What did Addy say they do? Talk about the issues they have with men? Something like that.

24

She punched the code in to turn off the security system and walked downstairs to open the door to Lara, Maya, and Addy. As she neared the door she also heard Shianne's voice and stifled an eye roll. Sometimes, Shianne was a bit much. But Lara loved her, and she could be fun.

Opening the door, she smiled at her friends, old and new, and stepped back as they entered.

Lara came in and gave her a hug, then stepped back and looked at her face. "Are you alright? I mean, I can see you've been beaten, and Tate warned me. But do you need anything?"

She chuckled. "No, I'm fine. I've been taking ibuprofen for pain and swelling, and I took a one-and-a-half-hour nap today. I felt much better after waking up."

Shianne stepped inside next. "Oh, my god." She stared, even leaning in and getting a nice close-up view. "How badly does it hurt?"

"It's actually not as bad as it looks, to be honest."

Lara grabbed Shianne's arm and tugged her up the

stairs as Maya and Addy crowded the entryway. She hugged them both briefly. "Nice to see you both. Thank you for agreeing to come here rather than meet out."

Maya grinned. "I don't care where I have a couple cocktails, as long as I do."

Addy giggled. "It's true. She doesn't care." Addy hugged her briefly, and she motioned with her arm for them to go up the stairs. She locked the door and checked it twice to make sure she'd locked it correctly. Her hands shook slightly. Inhaling a deep breath, she turned and saw Addy watching her.

Her cheeks burned. "I'm sorry. I just feel neurotic right now."

Addy nodded and stepped close. "It's normal. You've not only been through a savage beating, but you have an ex-boyfriend making you feel unsafe. Anyone in your same situation would feel the same way."

Her eyes watered slightly. "I only seem to feel safe when Spencer is here. I feel stupid saying this, but I locked myself in my bedroom after he left and didn't leave until Maya texted."

Addy linked an arm through hers and nodded. "Spencer is a great protector. Plus, his size alone makes him formidable. And he likes you, so that makes a difference, too."

She nodded, and they sauntered up the steps. "How do you know he likes me?"

Addy giggled. "It's impossible not to see it."

She swallowed the lump in her throat. What did that look like and how could others see it? She knew he wanted to have sex with her, but she didn't know he liked her. Well, the fact that he wanted to have sex with her would mean he liked her. But she wondered if it meant he *liked* her, liked her, or did he just like her and want to have sex with her? She would not ask Addy that question, but she wondered.

At the top of the steps she looked around at the food the ladies had laid out on the table. Then she saw the reusable containers sitting on the counter and realized Helissa probably packed them food.

Lara laughed. "Kenna, you should see your face. I mean, not the bruising, but the bewildered look. Didn't you notice the bags we were carrying?"

She shook her head. "No."

Lara shrugged. "It doesn't matter. We're all set up now, so let's grab some food to eat and mix some drinks. I'm tending bar for the first round. Call out your orders, ladies."

They took turns calling out for a glass of wine or a hard seltzer while she filled a plate with shrimp, and deviled eggs, and sliced beef, and cheese wedges, and veggies. She went to sit in the living room on the chair near the window, allowing three of them room on the sofa and another one to sit on the other side chair.

They sat and began eating, and Kenna vocalized her embarrassment. "I suppose we all would have been more comfortable at your place. There's so much room there."

Lara smiled. "It doesn't matter. This is very cozy. Is this your furniture or was it here?"

"It's mine. I moved it all back here since I don't know where I'll go next or when."

Maya grinned. "So you might not go back to Houston?"

"I don't know. I lost my job when my dad needed me to come back here. Without a job, I didn't want to keep my apartment there. It was terribly expensive to keep."

Shianne, never shy, asked, "How much is expensive?"

Lara admonished, "Shianne!"

Kenna laughed. "It's okay. I paid two thousand dollars a month."

"Holy crap!" Shianne exclaimed.

Lara shook her head. "My house payment isn't that much."

Kenna looked up at Lara. "That's right, you have a house. What did you do with it when you and Tate married and moved into the HOG?"

Lara shrugged. "I still have it. I thought I'd rent it out eventually, but I don't have the time to worry about it right now. So it's sitting empty."

Shianne shook her head. "I keep telling her she could get big bucks for an entire house."

"What would an entire house around here rent for?" Kenna asked.

Lara bit into a piece of beef and chewed. She finally answered, "I'm thinking of asking nine hundred a month. Renter pays all utilities."

"That's not a bad rental fee." Kenna said.

Loud pipes sounded outside and she glanced out the window. Colt drove by, slowing down near her place. She swallowed the dry knot in her throat and set the cheese in her fingers on her plate.

Maya stood and watched out the window, then looked at her. "Is that Colt's truck?"

All she could do was nod her head.

Maya pulled her phone up and tapped a few times.

"Maya, please don't call Spencer."

Maya's eyes locked on hers. "I'm not." She leaned forward. "I noted the time he drove by. But, for the record, Addy and I are as good at protection as Spencer. We wouldn't need to call him if something happened. We'd handle it."

Lara nodded. "Truth."

Kenna's cheeks heated. "I'm sorry. I didn't mean to assume you couldn't. I just wondered..."

"It's okay. We just want you to know you're safe."

"Thank you."

Maya winked at her and picked up her glass of wine. Kenna watched the beautiful woman take a sip of her wine and grin. "I can have a couple of drinks tonight, because Addy is actually the one on duty. And she's also our designated driver."

Addy nodded and took a drink of her water.

Shianne sat back on the matching chair to hers and took a drink from her wineglass. "Addy's my DD too."

Lara shook her head slowly, then turned to her. "So, tell us about Spencer."

Oh, her cheeks burned so hot she felt feverish. Her friends laughed. Lara leaned forward. "Busted."

"There's really nothing to tell." She fanned herself with her right hand and took a healthy drink from her wineglass, which made her friends laugh all the more. "He's been helping me."

Maya added, "Most 'protectors'..." she used air quotes, "...don't keep their hands at the small of their protectee's back. And he's kissed you, so that's more than just helping you."

"How do you know that?"

Addy, who had been quiet all this time, chimed in. "We're trained to pay attention to things. Surroundings, people, situations. We've all seen the signs."

Shianne leaned toward her. "He kissed you? Like once or more than once?"

Lara admonished Shianne once again. "Shianne. That's sort of personal."

"You're the one who asked about Spencer first, Lara."

"True, but I meant her feelings about him. Not the nitty-gritty details."

Shianne sat back, huffy. "Well, since I went on a date with him to the Bourbon Ball last year and he didn't so much as try to kiss me, I'm curious."

Kenna turned toward Shianne. "You went on a date with Spencer?"

"Yeah. Well, I don't think he wanted to go with me. It came about rather innocently enough. I was trying to get Lara and Tate together. We were all standing in the bakery and I mentioned Tate should take Lara to the Ball. Lara then said Spencer should take me. And that was all it was. Sadly. He's hot!"

Kenna grinned and nodded. "He is hot."

Maya finished her glass of wine and stood to refill her glass. "Anyone else need one?"

Colt drove by again, and Maya recorded the time on her phone. Lara turned to Maya. "Why didn't the police arrest him for the crap he pulled?"

"I don't know. That's a brilliant question for the sheriff. Especially since there's video of it."

Kenna's tummy rolled. "His father was always on the town board."

Shianne waved her hand in the air. "He still is. He's the president now and that mangy kid of his gets away with a ton of shit."

Kenna's phone signaled a text, and it unleashed butterflies in her tummy when she saw Spencer's name on the text.

"I'm checking in. How are you doing?"

She grinned as she replied.

"Good. The girls are here."

"Is Colt still driving by?"

"Yes."

She glanced at Maya, who was in a conversation about cookies with Lara at the moment.

"I'll finish here in a half hour."

Her heart fluttered. She knew what she wanted.

"I'd love for you to come here."

"See you soon."

25

Sawyer had the reports coming in from Maya and Remy. His anger rose to the surface at an alarming rate. Colt Lowe was proving to be a first-class ass and then some. His aches and pains aside, Kenna had been through enough without this asshole making her feel unsafe.

He finished up his job, left the construction site, and made a beeline for Kenna's place. Addy's car was still sitting in the parking area of The Paper Trail when he arrived, and he was grateful they were there with Kenna.

He sent off a quick text to Kenna to disarm the door for him, and the second he saw the "Disarmed" icon come up on his phone app, he entered the building, locked the door, and took the stairs as quickly as he could. His knees were still sore from diving away from Colt Lowe, preventing him from taking them two at a time.

At the top of the stairs, Kenna stood at the door and as soon as he saw her, he pulled her to his body for a hug. The warmth and feel of her body against his made his heart prance around in his chest. The sweet aroma of her perfume, oranges or citrus of some sort, filled his lungs and he inhaled it willingly.

"Are you alright?" he whispered.

"Yes." She turned toward the women in the living room, now watching them with interested grins.

He took her hand in his and walked toward them.

"Hey, ladies. Am I interrupting girls' night?"

Maya's amusement showed through, but to her credit, she only shook her head.

Shianne, of course, broke the silence. "It's good seeing you again, Spencer."

He wondered what she had said about their failed date. "Nice to see all of you."

Kenna squeezed his fingers. "Do you want a drink?"

"No. I'm good and if you want to continue trashing men or whatever, I can go hide in the bedroom."

"We're not trashing men." She giggled.

Maya leaned forward, her elbows on her knees, her hands clasped in front of her. "If I can get serious a moment."

He nodded, and she continued. "Colt Lowe. He's driven by here several times tonight, getting out of his truck and standing in the road staring up here once. He's getting bolder, and the sheriff isn't hauling his ass in."

"I saw your reports. I have a call into the sheriff asking just that question."

Addy stood. "I honestly think if you two want to get any sleep, and just for peace of mind, you need to bring Kenna to the HOG. Our team won't be split up that way and you'll be safe. Colt seems unpredictable, and he's escalating. On top of dealing with the BRR, play this smart."

He nodded. "I was going to talk to Kenna about that this evening, actually."

Colt's truck rumbled low again, this time on the First Street side of the building. Spencer descended the stairs, with Maya and Addy behind him. They watched out the window of the entryway as Colt's truck drove away.

He opened the door and stepped outside, scanning the area for anything Colt may have done. As he turned toward his truck, he saw the bright blue spray paint along the entire passenger side, and "Fucker" scrawled the entire length.

He bit his bottom lip as the expletives threatened to spew forth. Inhaling a huge breath, he turned to go upstairs, halted, and strode to see the side of Kenna's Jeep. The same blue paint on the side of her white Jeep said, "Slut."

"Dammit, I'm sick of this son of a bitch."

Maya snapped photos with her phone and Addy typed into hers, no doubt adding to the already voluminous reports on Colt Lowe.

He stomped up the stairs, three sets of eyes waiting for him in the kitchen. He sought Kenna's eyes. "I think we need to be at the HOG. The attacks are coming faster than we can keep up with and it's only a matter of time before you're here alone and I'm at work. Let's not give him the opportunity he's looking for."

"Okay. I'll pack some clothes."

She turned, Lara behind her, and they left him with Shianne staring at him. Her lopsided grin teased that something sassy was about to come out of her mouth and he braced himself. He wasn't in the mood.

"You two look good together," she said evenly.

"Thanks." Is that what he was supposed to say?

Shianne shrugged and traipsed down the hall after Kenna and Lara.

He went back downstairs to finish the setup of the security system so he could watch the building while they were at the HOG.

By the time Kenna, Lara, and Shianne stumbled down the stairs carrying a lot of luggage; he, Addy, and Maya were wrapping up the installation.

Addy brushed her hands together. "You're all secure now."

"Does that mean we aren't going to the HOG?"

He replied, "No, we're going. But I can keep a better eye on things here and catch Colt in action."

She nodded. He grinned as he held out his hand. "I need your phone for a second."

She handed it over and he opened her camera to take a picture of the bar code on the security system and set up the security app. The ladies began carrying the suitcases to the vehicles and Kenna pulled keys from her pocket to unlock the door to the office. "I need to grab work."

He followed her inside as she gathered up neatly organized piles of files. She moved gracefully and purposefully. She didn't look as stiff as she had this morning, which was progress in her healing. Her thick, long hair swayed as she moved, and his fingers itched to touch it.

She slid her paperwork into a briefcase and carried it to the door where he stood waiting for her. He bent briefly and kissed her lips before opening the door for her.

Spencer handed Kenna her phone and took the briefcase from her hand. Looking over her shoulder, he coached her. "Open the red icon." He studied her fingers as she touched her phone, taking in the red color on her perfectly shaped nails. "Now, tap on the Securetec icon."

He inhaled the aroma of her hair. "Now, see the various levels? Tap once on upper. Then tap Arm."

She followed instructions. "Now do the same for lower."

The word "Armed" appeared on her phone and she smiled. "Thank you."

"You're welcome." He stepped aside and let her pass him. She froze and he followed her gaze to the vehicles, silently chastising himself for not telling her about the paint job.

26

Kye pulled into the garage at the HOG in the space for guests. She tried keeping her eyes averted because every time she looked at her poor Jeep, she got mad all over again.

Inside the HOG, Spencer showed her the three guest bedrooms. She tilted her head up to look into his sexy eyes. "Where's your room?"

He chuckled and took her hand in his. Moving across the patio, he opened the door and stepped aside to let her enter. Inside his room, she inhaled the aroma of Spencer. His aftershave and shower soap filled the room with masculine scents and her nipples pebbled as she remembered how he felt on top of her earlier today. Gosh, that seemed like a lifetime ago already.

"I'd like to stay here with you," she whispered. He closed the door and gathered her in his arms in an instant. His lips found hers, his tongue slid into her mouth, his hands. Wow, his hands cradled her body into his body, all firm and muscular and sexy.

She wrapped her arms around his body and held him close as his hands roamed. He cupped the cheeks of her ass and squeezed them into his body, and her body reacted amazingly. Her nipples puckered tightly, which felt amazing pushed into his chest. She grew wet between her legs and her knees shook with excitement as he grew rigid against her.

His lips kissed down her jaw, then up to her ear. "I've thought about you all fucking day."

"Yeah," was all she could get out before his lips found hers again.

He walked her backwards until the back of her knees hit the bed. Then, he lifted her by grabbing her ass and hefting her up his body. She instantly wrapped her legs around his waist, and he slowly lowered them to the mattress.

His fingers worked the buttons on her blouse; her fingers worked on his zipper. As soon as his pants opened, her hand slid inside and cupped his length. He hissed out a breath near her ear, and she wrapped her fingers around his rigid cock. His breath left his body, and she savored the reactions coming from him.

He pushed against her as he whispered naughty, sexy things near her ear. "So fucking sexy. So many things I want to do for you. Thought about you all day. ...make you mine."

Her hand flew from his body to work at her own clothing. He helped her gently slide her blouse from her shoulders. His lips kissed a trail down her shoulder and to her breasts. He suckled her nipples, and she groaned and tugged at her pants. He chuckled. "Slow down, Kenna. We'll get there."

She stilled, liking the sound of his words, but she'd thought about him all day too.

He kissed her torso, stopping at the bruise on her ribs and kissing her there, before leaving a trail of dampness to the opening of her slacks and the lacy top of her panties.

His tongue traced across her abdomen before planting kisses in its wake. He lifted slightly and pulled her slacks over her hips, letting them drop to the floor before doing the same with her panties. He stood quickly, reached into his pants pocket, and dropped his pants to the ground, then his shirt flew off in a heartbeat.

He stared down at her, his eyes dark and sexy. His fingers whispered up the inside of her thigh and dipped into the curls between her legs. Her breath escaped her lungs in a whoosh as he swirled his fingers slowly around the area she wanted him to plunder. Raising her hips and moving under him to get his fingers where she wanted them, she moaned.

He chuckled a low, growly chuckle. "Maybe you'll like this better," he said as his mouth came down on her clit.

"Yesss," she whispered.

His tongue moved slowly over her clit, slowly down the seam of her pussy, then swirled around once again. His mouth was warm and soft as he suckled her. Kenna wavered between wanting to feel him inside of her to wanting his mouth to continue to bring her to orgasm. He sucked her clit into his mouth hard and she almost sat bolt upright. While he held her in his mouth, his first two fingers slid into her channel. "Ohh."

His fingers moved slowly in and out as his tongue and lips manipulated her clit. The assault on her senses made her dizzy, in the most delicious way. Her hands dug into his hair as he moved his mouth methodically and slowly. His fingers created sensations inside her body she'd never felt before. Never had she had a sexual encounter like this one.

His fingers moved faster, his mouth grew firmer on her sensitive tissues and as her breathing increased, so did the speed with which he moved. The fire inside of her built to a consuming heat and her vision blurred as her orgasm rolled through her. Spencer's lips sucked her in harder and she cried out his name when she let go.

His motions slowed, his lips softened, and her mind went blank.

He kissed his way up her torso, across her breasts, up her neck, to her ear where he whispered, "You're so fucking sexy, Kenna."

His movements were distracting for a moment, then the tip of his sheathed cock was at her entrance, and she opened her legs wider to let him in.

He slid in with ease and filled her so completely. He moved inside of her, his lips at her ear alternating between kissing them, to running his tongue around the shell of her ear to whisper how sexy she was. How good she felt. How amazing she was!

"Spencer," she groaned in his ear. "You feel so good inside of me."

He moved slightly faster now. He rotated against her sensitive clit, and it sent lightning bolts of pleasure through her body. Lifting himself up further, he stared into her eyes as he moved inside of her, their bodies moving together, the sounds of their lovemaking filling the room.

His movements became more urgent. Hers followed

suit. They moved together in unison, each racing to the finish line. She froze, pushed against him as a second orgasm rolled through her body, and he followed just moments later with a soft groan.

27

He woke with his arm wrapped around Kenna's shoulder, her back snuggled tightly to his front. He'd pressed his nose into her hair. Their legs were tangled together. Turning his wrist slightly, Spencer read five-fifteen on his watch.

Something had knocked the wind out of Colt's sails. For the past week and a half, he'd largely left her alone. She covered her bruising with makeup, and she felt less scared as the days passed. He enjoyed spending time with her. He looked forward to their days together, and he knew when he went to the construction site, she was safe here.

"Is it time to get up already?"

He kissed her head before she rolled over to snuggle her fabulous breasts into his chest. His cock moved, and she giggled. "I guess that answered my question."

He pulled her tighter to his chest. Not that there was much room between them anyway, but he loved the feeling of her body pressed to his. His hand slid down to her delicious bare bottom as he pulled her tighter to him there.

"You wake up naughty, Mr. Lawson."

"You make me wake up naughty, Ms. Lawrence."

Her arm circled his ribs and her hand splayed on his back. Then her hand roamed down his back to grab a handful of his ass. "Kenna, you'll need to finish what you start."

She giggled. "I'm good at finishing what I start."

"Prove it."

She lifted and rolled him onto his back, her body on top of his. She looked into his eyes. "This is how we first met."

"We had clothes on."

"Yes. Too bad about that but look at us now."

He chuckled, his hands grabbing a nice handful of her sexy ass. He grew rigid between them, and she wiggled her bottom, enticing him further.

With little effort, she lifted her bottom half until his cock bobbed up and she slid herself easily onto his cock.

"Fuck, that feels good." He groaned.

"I know."

She crawled on top of him, not full movements, just slow, lazy movements. He pushed her down onto him with his hands. She smiled a sexy lazy smile as he did. She was a tease, in the best way possible. They'd developed this routine since the first morning here and he enjoyed his mornings more than he ever dreamed he would.

Finally ready to get going, Kenna lifted herself up, her hands on either side of his head, her glorious breasts swaying as she moved on him. "That's more like it," he ruffed out as she seated herself fully on top of his cock.

Her lips turned up slightly, then she moved faster as they both grew more eager to finish what they'd started.

They'd stopped using condoms a few days ago since Kenna was on the pill. He liked this better.

She sat straight up on him, her hips moving faster and faster. He was helping her so he got the full effect of Kenna Lawrence, between her breasts dancing for him and her warmth wrapping his cock tightly.

Her eyes locked on his as she came closer to orgasm, her hands now on his chest to steady herself. His arms tightened as he lifted and dropped her down on his cock, his body grew damp and the tightness in his balls grew nearly impossible to bear just as they both let themselves go.

She fell onto his chest and he wrapped his arms around her until they both gained consciousness once again.

Finally, she lifted her head, kissed his chest and whispered, "Good morning."

He chuckled. "Good morning."

After they showered and before they left the room, he watched her dress in jeans and a white t-shirt, her dark hair trailing down her back.

"What do you have going on today?"

She looked up at him and smiled. "I want to see if I can visit Mom and Dad. I think I'm healed enough to see them now and share what happened without upsetting them too much."

"I don't want you going alone."

She straightened and stared at him. He braced for an objection, but when she spoke, it was actually what he should have been bracing for. "I'd love for you to meet my parents. Since we're obviously in a relationship, they should meet the man who rocks my world every day."

"We should probably leave that part out."

She laughed and continued pulling her tennis shoes on and tying them. "Are we in a relationship?"

He stood from his sitting position at the end of the bed and slid his fingers in the front pockets of his jeans. He locked eyes with her, his mind trying to determine what she was getting at.

"What do you think?"

"Well, we're having sex. Living together, sort of."

"And?"

Her head cocked to the right, and she crossed her arms in front of her. They stared at each other for a long time. At least it felt like a long time. "And what do you think?"

He stepped forward and grabbed the front of her t-shirt, pulling her to him. His arms wrapped around her body, essentially caging her in.

"What are you getting at here, Kenna? Does this feel like a relationship to you?"

She sniffed lightly and stared into his eyes. "I think so. But..."

He kissed her lips, softly. Then stepped back. "We should probably talk about this." He took her hand in his and pulled her to the foot of the bed. They sat side by side, hands clasped. He turned his head to look at her when he spoke. "We've fallen into an uncomplicated rela-tionship. It's easy because we're here, secluded behind the walls of the HOG. We're having great sex. We don't argue. It's been easy. It's been great."

"It has. But, I sense there's a but coming."

"Are you leaving? The state? Back to Houston?"

Her throat moved as she swallowed, and her body stiffened. "I don't know."

He nodded. "It's hard for us to move past where we are, without knowing there will be anything else."

28

His thumb smoothed circles into her palm as their fingers clasped together. She bit her bottom lip, happy that the cut had finally healed. She nodded her head, then looked into his handsome face. "You're right. That is the elephant in the room, isn't it?"

"I didn't think it was until a few minutes ago." He stood, letting go of her hand.

She swallowed the giant, dry, hard lump that had just formed in her throat. She started this. But she didn't want her parents to grow to like Spencer if they wouldn't stay together. He'd sort of just lobbed that ball into her court.

"Hey," he said above her.

She stood and took a deep breath. "Yeah. Sorry. I just worry about my parents. My dad's heart is still so weak and when I first brought it up, I was just being kind of funny. But it's not funny at all now, is it?"

"No. It's not funny." He hugged her close, and she wrapped her arms around his waist and closed her eyes.

He stepped back. "If you don't want me to go with you

to your parents, at least take one of the girls with you. Just, please, don't go alone. And let me know what you decide to do."

"Okay." She inhaled and tried keeping the tears at bay.

"I have to get to the construction site today, Kenna. The contractors have finished with the new walls and I have stuff to do."

"Of course," she croaked out. Clearing her throat lightly, she plastered on a smile and nodded. "I'll let you know."

She saw the sadness in his eyes when he nodded and turned to leave. He gently closed the door behind him. She reached back for a pillow and let herself cry into it. Once she'd gotten that out of her system, she laid the pillow in its place, fixed her makeup in the bathroom mirror and left the room to have breakfast before she got to work.

The laughter and chatter that filtered from the kitchen reached her ears before the delicious aroma of breakfast reached her nostrils. As she neared the coffeepot, she heard a chorus of good mornings and plastered that smile right back on her face before replying, "Good morning."

Her place next to Spencer was waiting for her, and she set her cup on the table and went to fill her plate from the food displayed on the counter. She picked a few slices of apple, a bit of scrambled eggs, and a couple of slices of bacon. She sat next to Spencer, who continued to eat his breakfast, and listened as Henry teased Maya about the video game they'd played the night before.

Spencer finished with his breakfast, then sat back to finish his coffee, and she was grateful when he wrapped his arm around the back of her chair. She glanced at him and smiled, but he didn't smile back.

Henry asked, "What's happening today?"

"I'm working on the new security system with the electrical contractor."

Henry finished his coffee. "Any bets on whether Colt actually shows up for work this week?"

Tate leaned forward. "I found out why he hasn't been there for a week. Turns out Baxter gave him a week off without pay because of his actions."

She looked at Tate, but he didn't look at her, so she continued to eat her breakfast. Her stomach didn't feel like eating. At all. But she didn't want anyone to know they'd had their discussion. And it left them both feeling rather blue. It was her fault. She shouldn't have said anything.

Maya addressed her. "Kenna, what do you have going on today?"

She swallowed her eggs. "I have a couple of documents to serve today. Then, I'm hoping to visit with my parents."

"How's your dad doing?"

"Mom says he's still weak. I feel bad that I didn't go there last week, but I didn't want him seeing me bruised and get upset."

"Yeah. That was likely a good call." Maya finished her coffee. "If you need anyone to go along with you on your service, just let me know. I'm off today."

"Thank you," she whispered. Her stomach clenched as Spencer stood. Luckily, Henry and Maya stood also, so it wasn't so obvious.

She stood with her plate and followed behind Spencer to the sink. He turned after she set her plate down, kissed her lips lightly and whispered, "Don't go without someone with you."

"Okay."

He nodded and left her standing by the sink, watching him walk away. That's when it hit her. Could she just leave now? What if her dad was doing much better and she could go somewhere else? Would she? As long as Colt was an issue, she wouldn't feel safe.

Her phone buzzed, and she pulled it from her back pocket. The number was a series of nines, but nothing else. She tapped the message, only to see a picture of her walking into her office a couple of days ago with Spencer. The text said,

"I'm always watching."

She closed the text, pocketed her phone, and rinsed her plate.

Maya came to stand beside her, coffee cup recently refilled, her back leaning against the counter. "So, what's up?"

Kenna rubbed her lips together, afraid if she spoke, the tears would burst forth again. She felt rather raw right now.

"I don't know."

"How can you not know?"

"I made the mistake of asking Spencer if we were in a relationship. I was kind of joking because I thought I should take him with me to see my parents. But he asked me if I still planned on leaving here when Daddy was better. I said I didn't know. And that seemed to put a damper on everything."

"Ugh. Yeah. I can see that it would." Maya sipped her coffee, then asked, "Well, would you?"

"I don't know. I'm not safe here with Colt. That's not a way to live."

"Right." Maya sipped at her coffee again as she stared across the room. "Did anyone ever tell you about Aidyn and Elena?"

"No. Only that he used to live here, but they went back to Indiana."

"Yes. Because it wasn't safe here for her because of Craig. It wasn't really safe here for Aidyn any longer either. Because of Craig."

"Right."

She turned and leaned her back against the counter like Maya.

Maya grinned. "You don't get it, do you?"

"Get what?"

"It doesn't have to be either-or. You can be safe here or not. You can be safe somewhere else with Spencer if you both want. Or, you can both work to make sure Colt isn't an issue and you can stay. There are options."

She stared at her friend. She was beautiful, with her olive skin and dark hair. Her sparkly brown eyes positively glittered sometimes when she was being a shit. Right now, her eyes were earnest. Maya shrugged, pushed off from the counter and moved away. "Just sayin."

29

The day drug by slower than a snail on a lazy day. He looked at his watch a million times during the morning hours. Then got sick of the time not moving and attempted to stop looking at his watch. Colt was absent from the job site again today, which made him comfortable and not. If he wasn't here, was he following Kenna? He hadn't left things that great with Kenna this morning, and that pissed him off. Why did the thought of her leaving cause a churning in the pit of his stomach? He knew when he first met her that she'd be leaving one day. He was protecting her and having fun in the meantime. But today when she asked if they were in a relationship, what the future could hold came flooding over him. And now he struggled to think of this as a little fun.

"Spencer?"

"What?" He looked over at the contractor he was working with on the security lines.

"I asked you if you got the wires run in the north wall."

He shook his head. "Oh. Yeah. I did."

"Okay. Why don't we take a break here? I've got some

emails to respond to and we've been at this for several hours now."

"Okay." As he strutted across the construction site, his phone buzzed. He pulled it from his back pocket and saw a text from a number that was all nines. Tapping it to open the message, he saw a picture of Kenna, taken today by the looks of her clothing. She was walking into Lara's bakery. The text said,

"I'm always watching."

Then the text disappeared. Poof. Gone from his phone. His brows furrowed together as he tried to retrieve it. He jogged to the construction trailer and pulled up his texts on his laptop. He ran all of his texts through the GHOST system, so hopefully, it had been captured.

The system opened painfully slowly and as he opened his messages, the image faded. He captured a screenshot of it. Though it had faded, he could still see the photo. Then his fingers scrolled, and he found Kenna's number.

"Hi."

"Where are you?"

"I'm at the office."

"Are you alone?"

She was quiet for a little too long and his stomach twisted.

"Kenna? Are you alone?"

"Yes."

He let out a shaky breath. "Did you go to Lara's today?"

"You're behaving just like Colt."

"I'm nothing like Colt. You should certainly know that by now. I got a text just a few minutes ago of a picture of you walking into Lara's today."

He heard movement and the squeak of a chair. Then she replied, "I'm sorry."

"I'll come and get you and follow you home."

"No." He heard her huff out a breath. "Don't do that. It's alright. I'm locked inside here and I have a little work to do. I'll be at the HOG in about an hour."

"Kenna." He swallowed and tried to get his stomach to stop twisting so he could catch his breath. "I'm sorry about this morning. I don't know why I let it get so heavy."

"I am too. My stomach has been in knots all day."

"Mine too."

He could hear her sniff on the other end of the line and his heart felt like it was being squeezed by an iron fist. "Stay there. I'll be there in a few minutes."

"Spencer. You don't have to come. I probably need..."

"I'll be there." He ended the call and heaved out a deep breath. The first thing he did was look up Colt's address. Tonight, he'd sneak out to Colt's place and put a tracker on his truck.

He closed the lid on his computer and tucked it into its bag. He texted Henry to tell him he was heading out for the day and got a thumbs-up.

He jumped in his truck, which he'd just gotten back from the dealership, blue paint removed, and turned toward The Paper Trail.

He observed Kenna's Jeep between the buildings, the paint had been removed, and released a breath. He pulled in behind her Jeep and jumped from his truck. He marched swiftly to the porch and rapped on the door so she could open it.

She opened the door for him. Her face was pale, drained of all color. Her eyes were round and filled with fear.

He stepped inside, locked the door, and pulled her to his body for a hug. Her body shook as he held her.

"What's happened?"

She inhaled deeply, then he stepped back, and she pulled him toward her computer. There, she had an email open, and the picture was of her, beaten and bruised from a couple of weeks ago. It said, "I love looking at you like this."

He clamped his jaw tightly. Clicking the sender's email address, it came up with an "Error, not found" message. He emailed the GHOST and RAPTOR server and wrote a message. "Cyber, please see if you can tell where this email came from. Spencer."

He closed the lid on her computer, then stood. Kenna stood frozen, staring at her computer like it would reach out and grab her. He pulled her into his body and wrapped his arms around her. "I'm here for you."

"Okay," she whispered into his chest. He rested his chin on her head and stared off across the room. After a long moment, she pulled away slightly. "I promised my parents I'd come for dinner."

"I'll go with you."

Her lips formed a straight white line, then she took a deep breath. "Okay."

"Look, this morning caught me off guard. I wasn't expecting the question, and I wasn't expecting to have to think about you leaving this soon. I enjoy being with you. I enjoy being around you. I'm not ready for you to go. It hit me like a punch from Rocky Balboa."

"I shouldn't have put you on the spot. I'm sorry. I'm not ready to leave you either. But..." she pointed to her computer. "I'm not safe here."

30

Kenna held her mom close for a long time. It felt good to hug her close. "Mama, this is Spencer Lawson. He's been helping me. Spencer, this is my mama, Niya Lawrence."

Her mom nervously asked, "Oh dear, do you have so much work you need help? Don't let your father know this, Kenna." Her mom then looked up at Spencer and smiled brightly. "It's nice to meet you, Spencer."

"It's nice to meet you, Niya."

Her mom nervously tittered about. "Come in, come in, please. Sit down. What can I get you to drink?"

Kenna laughed. "Mama, sit and talk to us." Kenna opened the refrigerator and pulled a beer and a hard seltzer from inside. She set the beer in front of Spencer and smiled at him. He winked at her and that felt so good. Almost like they were back where they'd been before this morning's awfulness. "Mama, do you want something besides coffee?"

"No, honey. Coffee for me."

She poured her mom a cup of black coffee and sat

next to Spencer at the table and across from her mom. "How's Daddy doing?"

Her mom frowned slightly, then inhaled a deep breath. "He's not good, honey."

"What does the doctor say?"

"You know. The usual. He's old, his heart is bad and get your things in order."

Kenna frowned. "Have Sean and Jonathon come to see him?" She turned to Spencer. "I'm sorry. Sean and Jonathon are my younger brothers. They don't live around here anymore. Sean moved to Tennessee and Jonathon lives in Florida."

"I've told them he isn't well. I haven't told them the last."

"You need to, Mama. They need to know. They should come home and say goodbye."

Her mom teared up and Kenna reached across the table to take her hand. "Mama."

Her mom shook her head and pulled a tissue from the pocket of her blouse. She dabbed at her eyes and cleared her throat. The oven timer went off, and she stood to remove a casserole from the oven. Kenna got up and pulled four plates from the cupboard.

"Only three, honey."

"Mama. Isn't he eating?"

"Not much these days."

She turned and saw Spencer watching them. He stood and gently took the plates from her hands. "Go see him."

Her bottom lip quivered, but just looking into his eyes gave her strength. She nodded and moved toward her parents' bedroom. Her mom said behind her, "Spencer honey, I'm sorry. Please help yourself."

Dread filled her belly as she neared the door to her

parents' bedroom. Twisting the knob, she slowly opened the door and saw her father reading something in bed. At first glance, he looked fine. But, as she neared, and he didn't even notice her presence, her shoulders tensed and her stomach flipped.

"Daddy," she whispered.

He didn't seem to hear her. She moved closer to him and laid her hand on his shoulder. He startled, his eyes wide when he saw her. "Kenna, honey. Nice to see you. Why didn't you say something when you came into the room?"

"I'm sorry, Daddy."

She pulled the chair in the corner closer to the bed and sat facing him as her mom sat on the edge of the bed.

"Are you hungry, Daddy?"

"Your mama fed me a bit ago."

"Okay. How are you feeling?"

His lips quivered, and she saw the expressions fly across his face. In the end, he pretended everything was fine. "I'm doing so much better."

It made her sad. So sad that at the end he was going to pretend it wasn't.

His shaky hand reached out for hers and she held his as she watched his eyes dim. "How's business Kenna? Everything alright?"

"It is. I'm taking good care of it for you to come back. You don't have to worry about a thing."

He smiled, his eyes seemed unable to focus. "I knew you would take the best care of it for me. You always did."

He squeezed her hand, then rested his head back against the headboard. "I'm tired, honey."

"Okay." She stood and kissed his forehead. Pushing the chair back to its corner, she listened as her mom settled her dad, moving the magazine he pretended to read just moments before.

Solemnly she ambled to the front of the house, where Spencer sat in a side chair, watching out the window, looking as sexy as he ever had. His long legs, bent at the knee, expressed just how tall he was. She stifled a sigh as she observed his broad chest filling the chair as it had never been filled. She wanted to climb into his lap and let him hold her for hours.

His eyes met hers as she entered the room and he held his hand out to her as if he had read her mind. She stepped into his space, and he gently pulled her down onto his lap and wrapped her in his arms. She rested her head on his strong, massive shoulder and inhaled his aftershave. "Thank you."

"You're welcome."

She felt his voice rumble through his chest and took comfort in it. His arms held her tight, his body protected her from the world, his presence filled her with hope and light and love.

Her mom entered the room and sighed. "That looks very nice."

Kenna sat up, her cheeks flushed, but her mom dismissed her movement with a wave and sat on the sofa across the room. "I fell in love with your father the moment I met him. Our eyes landed on each other across the room. We were at a church social and the boys were on one side of the room and the girls on the other. Only the brave boys would make the walk across the floor to ask a girl to dance, so we usually watched each other from afar. He was brave. He never looked away from me as he stepped across the room. He bent at the waist, and when he stood up, he asked, 'Would you care to dance with me?'

For a few moments, I couldn't say anything. This brave boy who I'd been watching from afar asked me to dance. I wasn't the prettiest girl in the room, that went to Janice Furlong. But he asked me. When I finally found my voice, and said, "Yes, please." He held his arm out for me to place my hand in the crook of his arm and led me to the middle of the dance floor. We danced the rest of the night. Every song." Her voice trailed off and Kenna brushed tears from her eyes.

"That's a great story, Niya. I'll bet you're wrong, though. I'll bet you were the prettiest girl in the room that night." Spencer softly replied.

Her eyes landed on Spencer, and she watched her mom's cheeks tint pink. A lone tear fell from her mom's eye and left a trail of wet down her cheek until it fell on her blouse. She softly repeated, "We danced every dance." She swiped at her cheek, then sniffed. "We married three months later. We've been married for close to forty years. I've never kissed another boy. It's only been him." Her mom looked into her eyes for a long time. "I'm going to miss him so much. Don't waste your time, Kenna. Grab every minute you can and hold on to it until it squeals."

31

The drove her home. He held her hand. They'd eaten dinner with her mom. Cleaned up the kitchen, and Renna stepped into her father's room to say good night.

She inhaled deeply. "How did your parents meet?"

He chuckled. "Much differently than yours. My mom was good friends with Jax Sager, Maya and Myles's mom. Mom had a boyfriend who she'd found out was deep into trafficking. He'd roped her into helping him and when he found out she'd dug into his business, he threatened to kill her. She called Jax, because Maya is just like her mom. Strong, fearless, take charge, the real deal. Jax told her to get to Indiana. She was on assignment, but Jax called my dad, who owed her a favor, and asked him to pick up my mom from the airport. When he got to the airport, this poor, beaten, bedraggled woman got off the plane and his protective instincts reared up. He got her back to the compound and into the medical treatment room and began cleaning up her wounds. Apparently, one of her boyfriend's goons had gotten to her before she could get away. But, luckily, she got into her car and got to the airport. Mom asked Dad to teach her how to protect herself, so she never felt vulnerable again. He did. During that time, they fell in love."

"It almost sounds like us." He glanced at her, then pulled her hand to his lips and kissed her fingers.

"Sort of. I believe you threw yourself at me, though."

Her mouth fell open, then snapped shut. "Uh, no. You ran right for me and grabbed me in your arms and we fell to the ground together."

He laughed. "Something like that."

He pulled the truck into the garage and turned off the ignition. "I'm sorry about your dad, Kenna. I want you to know that."

She swallowed and nodded. "Thank you."

He opened his door and strode around the truck, opened her door and held his hand out to help her down.

They walked hand in hand into the HOG. It was quiet inside, as if everyone had gone out for the night, except all the vehicles were in the garage.

Loud voices filtered in from outside and he grinned. "They're outside playing something. We can either join them or watch some television."

"Oh, it's been such a gut-wrenching day today. How about we join them and have some fun?"

He leaned down and kissed her lips. "That's what I hoped you'd say."

He pulled her to the door, and they exited through the garage and out onto the side yard where his friends were playing volleyball.

"Hey, there they are. Come join us." Addy yelled.

Spencer pulled his t-shirt off so he matched the rest of the guys and she ran to the side where Addy, Lara,

Shianne, and Maya were playing. Maya laughed, "We're kicking their asses."

"Really?"

"Really. They can't move worth a shit. We're limber and vicious. Don't give them any breaks." Maya snapped back.

"Vicious mode activated." She mocked.

Their volleyball game got cut-throat but the entire time it was fun. They'd worked up a sweat and now they sat around a fire outside, having a drink and chatting. It felt good. The girls' team won, though he still couldn't figure out how they did that. The guys were much stronger and taller, but those little ladies kicked their asses.

Spencer stood. "I'm taking a shower." He walked into the HOG, his heart feeling lighter than he felt this morning. His phone buzzed, and he looked at the text that came in from Piper at RAPTOR.

Opening the text, it read,

> "I'm sorry it's taking us a while. This person is pretty good at encryption. We're still working on it. I just wanted you to know."

He sent a text back,

> "Thank you."

And continued on to his room. He hadn't gotten to Colt's house last night to install a tracker. He'd have to see if time lent itself tomorrow. Maybe by then, they'd have more answers.

Warming the water, he pulled out clean underwear

and sleep pants, then happily shrugged off his sweaty jeans and dropped them into the hamper.

Letting the warm water slide down his body, his mood lifted even further as soft, warm hands slid up his body. He looked into her eyes, which had darkened to emerald green, and her soft lips, which she licked and it made his cock hard.

"Is this make-up sex?"

"I suppose it is."

"Good. I've heard make-up sex is the best."

"Me too."

He kissed her, nipping at her bottom lip as his hands roamed her body, slick with water and soft.

He grabbed both of her wrists in one of his hands and pulled them up over her head. The devilish smile that formed on her lips spurred him on. He turned her body, so she faced the wall, holding her hands high. He kneed her legs open and with his left hand, he pulled her body so her ass stuck out nice and pretty.

"You're so fucking sexy, Kenna," he husked.

He pumped his cock several times until he was good and hard. First, he slid his fingers into her body, getting her ready, then he slid his cock into her body, nice and slow. Her head fell forward, and he heard her moan. "You like that?"

"Yes," she whispered.

He reached around her with his left hand and rubbed her clit until he could feel her body shake.

He let her hands go, making sure she held herself against the wall with them, then he grabbed her hips in his hands and moved in and out of her fast and furious. Their bodies slapped together, and he could see her beautiful breasts swinging as he pounded into her again and again.

She cried out, "Spence," as she orgasmed and he wrapped both of his arms around her and pulled her back tightly as he whispered in her ear, "Kenna."

She woke up with her back pushed tightly to Spencer's front, their legs tangled together and his nose in her hair, his arms around her body. It was the best way to wake up for sure.

He twisted his arm to look at his watch. She saw it was just after five.

He rolled her over onto her back, and she slowly opened her eyes all the way. He kissed her lips. "We're in a relationship."

She giggled. "I knew it when you knocked me over and held me tight."

He shook his head and twisted to get out of bed.

"Where are you going? Aren't we going to have sex?"

"Honey. I love that you think like that, but this morning I need to talk to Tate about the email and text."

She swallowed and sat up. "Spencer." She watched him turn toward her. His naked body was a sight to behold. All of it. Yum. "I got a text too. I didn't tell you."

"What did it say?" He slipped on his briefs and sat on the edge of the bed.

"It was a picture of me walking into the office after they beat me up. It said, "I'm always watching.""

He rubbed his face with his hands, his back became rigid. "When did you get it?"

"Yesterday morning, after you left for work."

He scraped his hand through his hair, and his face grew hard. His jaw tightened. "I need to see your phone."

She pulled it from the nightstand and unplugged it. "It disappeared. I looked for it again yesterday and it's gone. So, I wondered if I imagined it."

He scrolled through her phone and saw nothing from anyone that looked suspicious. "Did the number it came from have all nines in it?"

"Yeah."

"I need to take this so we can do a forensic examination of it. I can get you a burner phone if you need it."

"I'm not going anywhere today, except my parents'."

"Take someone with you, honey. Promise me."

"I will."

"I'll get you a burner phone until I can get this one back to you."

She watched him dress. His body was drool worthy. He was honest to god, well, a god. He could model for the Greek gods. And she was falling in love with him. Hard. Real hard.

She scooted off the bed and slipped her panties on, and her jogging pants over the top. Grabbing her bra from the back of the chair, she slipped her arms into it and hooked it in the back. She pulled one of Spencer's t-shirts from his top drawer.

"I have to go back to my place and get some clean clothes."

"Have Helissa wash your clothes."

"I can't do that." She watched him from across the room.

"Then you do it. The laundry room is here for everyone."

Taking a moment to think about it, she asked, "Does Helissa do your laundry?"

Slipping a t-shirt over his head, he responded, "Yeah. She does everyone's laundry."

Spencer turned and looked at her. As in, up and down, his eyes looking over every part of her. It was sexy. He took three strides to reach her. His arms wrapped tightly around her body and lifted her feet off the ground. His lips planted on hers, their tongues dancing, their lips moving and tasting. His head pulled back, and he stared into her eyes. "The offer of sex? Keep that on the agenda for today. But your safety comes first. Yeah?"

She smiled. How could she not when he said things like that? "Yeah."

"Also, don't go anywhere alone. Please. I think Addy's off today."

"Okay."

He kissed her again, this time not as in-depth, but a great kiss nonetheless. He set her on the ground, kissed the top of her head, snagged her phone off the bed and in a swoosh, he was out the door.

She took a deep breath and glanced at the clock on the bedside table. It had only been twenty minutes since her eyes opened and already it felt like an entire day.

Gathering their clothing and tossing them into the hamper in the bathroom, she'd wash his too. She carried the hamper out to the kitchen, then to the laundry room.

She sorted their clothing, started the first load and exited the room, closing the door behind her.

Helissa smiled at her when she exited, and Kenna felt kind of funny taking on one of her jobs. "Good morning."

She returned Helissa's smile. "Morning. I hope you don't mind me doing laundry."

Helissa shook her head. "I don't mind at all. This is your home. Use what you like."

"Well, not really. I mean, it's not really my home."

Helissa's brows lifted and disappeared behind her dark bangs. But, to her credit, she said nothing further on the subject.

"Breakfast is ready, Kenna. Help yourself. Some others have come and gone."

"Thank you." She filled a coffee cup, added creamer—Irish cream this morning and set it on the table. She went back to the counter and filled her plate. Hash browns, scrambled eggs, and fresh fruit. Every morning was like a buffet at a hotel, only the food was good and fresh.

She sat at the table alone, feeling lonely and kind of weird. Addy entered the kitchen and Kenna felt instantly better. Addy filled her plate and poured coffee, then sat across from her.

"What do you have planned today?" Addy asked.

"I'm planning to go to my parents', and I have two people to serve. Spencer said I can't go alone, and I hoped you'd join me."

Addy chuckled. "He told me. I'm at your service."

She shook her head. These people communicated with ease. "Thank you, Addy."

Addy giggled and took a bite of an apple.

Tate and Spencer entered the kitchen. Spencer sauntered over and laid a cell phone next to her. "Our numbers are all programmed in this phone. You can add your parents and only give them this number. While we have your phone today, if any business calls come in, we'll forward them to this number. We're monitoring both phones now."

She swallowed. "Okay. Where is my phone?"

Tate answered, "It's in my office hooked to my computer. We're running some scanning software on it to see if we can locate the text that disappeared in the metadata. Then we'll see if we can trace it. I've got Spencer's phone and running the same thing on it."

She turned to Spencer. "I thought you captured the text on your phone."

"I only got a screenshot as it was fading."

"Oh."

She took a deep breath. Spencer sat next to her and turned her chair to face him. "We're doing everything we can to figure this out. But it's important you stay with Addy today and only go where you need to go. Do you absolutely have to effect service today on those parties?"

She slowly shook her head. "No. I just like to do it right away. Neither of these are something that has to be done today."

"Kenna. Honey, please don't work today. Right now, we don't know where Colt is or even if it is Colt."

Her brows bunched together. "Who else could it be?" She stared into Spencer's eyes.

His were steady and his face was calm when he replied. "It could be Kent Bennit."

"Why would he do that? I thought he was working with you all to create peace."

"He is. But we know he has computer skills, and he's used them similarly in the past. Plus, you served him with papers suing him, so he may have taken that as a slap in the face."

"I'm not suing him. Someone else is."

"We know, honey. But sometimes people aren't rational."

She turned to Addy, who watched silently as they spoke. Her face was unreadable.

Kenna took a deep breath and let it out slowly.

Spencer leaned in and kissed her quickly. "Tate, Henry, and I have to go out for a while. Don't be gone long, please."

She nodded as he turned her chair back to the table. When she lifted her head, she saw the three men exiting into the garage. Her eyes landed on Addy's and she shrugged. "I guess you're stuck with me today."

Addy grinned. "We'll make the best of it."

Sheppard took him around the new building several times; he measured, adjusted the cameras and measured again. Tate was in the construction trailer speaking to Baxter about the next steps and Henry was walking the perimeter again. They all felt as though the BRR was about to strike and they didn't know where or how. But something was up.

He heard an old truck nearing the base from the mountains and he strained to watch which direction it went once it reached the county road.

As it turned toward the construction site, he moved forward toward the truck. He pulled his phone from his back pocket and tapped Henry's number.

"What's up?"

"BRR truck just pulled into the lot."

"I'm on my way."

Rounding the building, he saw Gerard and Jasiah Weston alight from the truck. Gerard called to him as he neared.

"Spencer, we came to speak with you."

"Okay. What's on your mind?"

"We'd like the power brought up the mountain. I know it's something the town has to approve, but we're six months into our negotiations and all we've seen from it is our citizens are finding jobs and working to pay the taxes, but we're offered nothing in return. It's one thing that has Craig stewing right now."

Spencer's jaw tightened. They had a lot of nerve. Henry approached and Tate exited the construction trailer and came toward them. "Have you spoken to him about the beating Kenna took?"

"We have. We told him what you said about workers needing to feel safe. He says he understands."

"It doesn't matter that he understands, Gerard. It matters that he never does anything like that again," he ground out.

Jasiah lifted his hands in front of him. "Spencer, we're trying. Honestly, we are. This is too much change happening too quickly. Craig isn't on board with any of it and forcing it on him all at once has him on the defensive all the time."

"Well now, we're on the defensive, too. Why would we send anyone up there to work if they don't know if they'll come down the mountain without being beaten? Or worse?"

Gerard looked briefly at Jasiah. Jasiah nodded and Gerard took a deep breath. "We've been speaking with our people, privately. We feel we have enough people to support Craig's removal as president."

Spencer's stomach tightened. He stared at both Gerard and Jasiah in disbelief. "What does that look like?"

Jasiah spoke slowly and clearly. "We'd have to put him in jail, most likely."

Tate chuckled. "For what?"

Gerard swallowed and shuffled his feet. "We have witnesses that saw him kill Faye, Kent's mother."

Spencer's jaw tightened again. His eyes slid to Tate's, and they stared at each other for a few moments. Tate finally said, "Witnesses aren't proof. They're good and, provided they are credible, it could work. But we're going to have all kinds of issues with this. First, to get him to trial, he's entitled to an impartial jury of his peers. The townspeople aren't necessarily his peers and your people aren't impartial. The townspeople aren't impartial either."

Gerard's head dropped. "We're trying to figure this out. But we need some action from you to show you're sincere with your promises."

Tate nodded and glanced at him once again. It conflicted Spencer. Yes, he was pissed the fuck off. Craig had beaten Kenna. He wanted to run his fist right into Craig's face several times. But if Gerard and Jasiah were earnest, they were trying.

Spencer asked, "What's Kent been up to all this time?"

Jasiah's head jerked at the change in topic, his brows furrowed as he stared back.

Spencer relaxed his jaw, and Henry shifted next to him. "He's been working at CyberSecure. He's started a few days ago. To our knowledge, he's been working every day."

Spencer swallowed. That was easy enough to check out. And, the fact he worked at a computer security store could also be a way for them to check and see if he's sent any disappearing texts.

Gerard sighed. "Why are you asking about Kent?"

Tate stepped in, "We've had some interesting things happen, electronically, in the past few days and we're trying to figure out who and why. That's all."

Gerard shook his head. "Kent feels bad about his actions in the past. He's trying real hard to make up for it. To my knowledge, he's giving his entire paycheck, minus only fuel for his car, to the BRR to help pay for the taxes. Then, he's said, he'll work to pay for the damages he caused."

Jasiah shook his head. "Not every bad thing that happens down here is our fault."

Spencer looked into his eyes. He didn't see deception; he saw genuine sadness and frustration.

Taking a deep breath, he turned to Tate. "How about this? If Gerard and Jasiah can guarantee safety for me and another man, we can begin running wires. We can start with a mini substation just over there." He pointed to a flat spot up the side of the hill, just off the road. "The mini-sub can't power homes, and the wires aren't run yet anyway, but it can be the start. If we can get Casper to speak with the governor of Kentucky, perhaps we could begin with a joint effort of the Department of Defense and the State of Kentucky to bore into the mountain, to set up anchors for lines. The bulk of the cost will be the boring. If we can have that paid for in tandem, we can then run power lines up for the homes. We'll work with those who cooperate first." He looked at Gerard and Jasiah. "But you need to provide a secure environment for them to work."

Tate nodded and turned to Gerard and Jasiah. "What do you say to that?"

Jasiah nodded. "We can provide the security. Some of our men haven't found jobs yet. They can fulfill the security aspect of it."

Spencer reached forward and shook Jasiah's hand. "That's a great start. And, beginning immediately, Craig's men guarding the roads has to end."

Gerard reached forward and shook hands with each of them. "I can guarantee that."

Tate added, "Let's begin having weekly meetings to share information and ideas and simply to stay in contact to bridge this gap."

Spencer's heart raced. This was good. This was very good. They may actually begin to see some progress in this new pact with the BRR.

Tate slapped him on the back. "Nice job, Spence."

"Thanks."

Henry nudged him and grinned as he walked toward the construction trailer.

Spencer swallowed and watched Gerard and Jasiah get in their truck and drive up the hill. Now they'd have to hope Casper would agree to negotiate with the powers that be to help them with this peace deal.

Henry chuckled. "I have news."

"That right? What kind of news."

"The sheriff called a few minutes ago to tell us they found the kid who cut the wires. Baxter was right, it was a hazing. He's a freshman this year and the football team was making him earn his place on the team."

"At least we know that much." He scraped his hands through his hair. "And we know it wasn't the BRR."

Tate added. "The sheriff also told us they've spoken to Colt. He's agreed to back off. Apparently, he's been to anger management counseling, and he's agreed to go back to refresh himself on dealing with his issues."

"That's it? That's all that will happen?" he barked.

Shrugging, Tate said, "It doesn't seem right, but we know the law is lax here."

Kenna answered the phone ring. "Hello?"

"Hi, Mama. How are you and Daddy today?"

"Kenna, honey, did you get a new phone number?"

"Yes. Sort of. It's temporary."

"Oh, okay."

"I'd like to come out to the house and see you and Daddy today."

He again hesitated a moment. "Yes, I think you better. I don't think he has long, honey.

Her heart hurt. It felt like a physical blow. Tears formed instantly, and she struggled to suck in a breath. She whispered, "Okay. I'll be right there."

"See you soon, honey."

She ended the call and turned to Addy. "He's not doing well."

Addy stood. "Let's get going then."

She swallowed a lump the size of a softball and stood. "Addy. Can I bring my laptop with me? I'm thinking my brothers won't get here in time and I could video call them so they can talk to Daddy before he...." She swallowed several times.

Addy stepped into her space and hugged her. "I'm not sure if Tate has finished with your laptop, but we can surely bring mine."

"Thank you."

Addy left the kitchen and Kenna strode through the house, toward her bedroom to change clothes. She quickly put on a pair of navy-blue trousers, the bruises on her legs still present, though fading away. She donned a thin, white summer sweater. She gathered her hair into a ponytail and brushed it out until it gleamed, but then remembered that her father liked it when it was down around her shoulders. She pulled the hair tie out of her hair and brushed her hair once again, letting it fall over her shoulders.

You're wasting time, she admonished herself.

Addy drove while she texted Sean and Jonathon.

"Daddy's not doing well. I'm on my way there with a laptop so you can speak to him via video, in case he doesn't make it until you get here."

Her brother Sean was the first to respond.

"Okay. I got a flight out at five this evening."

"Okay. I'll let him and Mama know."

"I'm hurrying, Kenna. Love you."

She smiled. She always chided him on being too slow. Jonathon responded a while later.

"I'm on my plane now. Will be there in two hours."

"Okay,"

she responded.

Addy pulled into her parents' driveway, and she sucked in a deep breath. Already it felt like a house of mourning. Even the flowers outside looked sad.

Addy turned her head and smiled. "Are you ready, Kenna?"

She looked into her friend's beautiful brown eyes and tried to smile, but even she could tell it was fake. "Yes. And no. Is that bad?"

"It's not bad at all. I'll be with you."

She could only nod as her eyes filled with tears once again. It was a pattern she didn't like.

They walked side by side to the kitchen door just off the carport. She twisted the handle and opened the door, surprised it wasn't locked.

"Mama." She called out softly, so she didn't disturb her father if he was sleeping.

Her mom appeared from the bedroom down the hallway. She met her mom halfway and wrapped her in a warm embrace.

Her mom kissed her temple then smiled. "How are you this morning?"

"I'm good." Her mom looked behind her to Addy. "You didn't bring your handsome young man today."

"He has to work. This is my friend Addy. Adelaide Masters. Addy, this is my mom, Niya."

Addy stepped forward and wrapped her mom in a sweet embrace. "It's nice to meet you, Niya."

"It's nice to meet you too, Addy." Her mom smoothed the front of her blouse, her hands shivering.

"Mama. How are you? How's Daddy?"

Her mom's lips quivered slightly, and Kenna wrapped her arm around her mom's shoulders.

"I'm as fine as I can be. Daddy won't be with us much longer. He's barely woken up today. The doctor is on his way out here."

"Let's go see him. Sean and Jon are on their way home."

Her mom's sad face turned to her. "They won't make it, honey."

She swallowed again and turned to Addy. Addy nodded slightly and held her hand as they made their way down the hallway and to her dad's bedside.

The room looked exactly as it had last night. Everything was right where it always was. Except her father was lying down on the bed now, his grayish pallor stark against the crisp white pillowcase. His mouth hung open and his chest barely rose and fell with his breaths.

Kenna inhaled as she sat on the edge of the bed, near her father. She picked up his still hand and held it between hers.

"Hi, Daddy."

His eyes fluttered but didn't focus. Addy stepped near her and whispered in her ear. "He can hear you. Keep talking."

She looked into Addy's kind eyes. It made her eyes water all the more.

Her voice cracked. "Daddy." Kenna cleared her throat and tried once more. "Daddy. How are you feeling today?"

His eyes fluttered open, and his mouth moved, but no sound came out. She glanced at Addy, who nodded her encouragement. Her mom sat at the foot of the bed and rubbed her father's feet. Addy sat in the chair in the corner. There for support if she needed, but not too close.

"Daddy. I met a boy. He's just the best, and he takes such good care of me. He's so strong and handsome. He's wonderful and I've never felt more loved. I'd love for you to meet him. His name is Spencer and I know you'll be best friends."

Tears streamed down her face, but she continued. "Jon's on his way home. He's excited to see you. Sean is too. After they visit with you, I'll introduce you all to Spencer. I'm sure the boys will have to give him a hard time, like they did with other boys over the years. Remember when they teased Doug, my eighth-grade crush? That poor boy didn't know what to do."

Her mom chuckled behind her. "They sure made his life a living hell for a few days."

She sniffed and nodded. "They sure did."

She turned back to her father. She pulled her phone out of her pocket and dialed Sean's number.

He answered, "I can't get there any sooner, Kenna."

She cleared her throat. "You need to talk to Daddy now, Sean. You may not have the chance later. I'm putting the phone by Daddy's ear."

She listened as Sean told her dad how much he loved him. How he taught him so much and set him on the right path in life and how there was no other father in the world better than he was. She used three tissues and was reaching for another when Sean called out, "Kenna."

She pulled her phone up to her ear. "Yes. I'm here."

Sean's voice cracked. "Thank you. See you later." As Kenna ended the call she heard Sean's muffled sobs.

35

Spencer turned the stove and followed Tate to his office. Friday had been quiet after Gerard and Jaziah left. They'd done a search and checked out Cyber-Secure's site. Cyber security companies had to register with certain agencies for bonding and other legal securities, since they usually had access to sensitive information. They'd crosschecked several sites and still had the email Kenna had received running through some forensic metadata checking. Nothing surfaced on CyberSecure. And, as he thought about it, it was highly unlikely that they would give Kent, on his first day on the job, carte blanche to access any systems that he could then use to scrub data from emails.

Kent probably wasn't their culprit, but better safe than sorry where Kenna's safety was concerned.

Tate sat at his desk and picked up Kenna's phone.

"We got it."

Spencer walked around Tate's desk and looked over his shoulder. The text Kenna had received was populating on the screen, a bit pixelated, but hopefully it would settle in and develop clearly.

Spencer picked up his phone, still plugged into Tate's computer, which was running the software scan on it, and his text was populating too.

"Here too."

"Good. As soon as they come through completely, we'll get the number from the sender."

He set his phone down, excited to tell Kenna what they'd found. He pulled up his burner phone and texted her.

"Where are you?"

Within a few seconds, she responded.

"Mom and Dad's."

"How is he?"

"He's dying. The doctor said it won't be long now."

"I'll be right there."

To Tate he said, "Kenna's dad is passing. I'm headed out there to be with her."

"I'm sorry, Spencer. Let me know if there is anything we can do."

His stomach tightened as he drove to the Lawrences' home, just on the outskirts of town. Addy's car and another car were in the driveway. He parked behind Addy's car and hustled to the door that led to the kitchen.

He knocked softly, then stepped inside without waiting, eager to get to Kenna. He heard soft whispers down the hallway and followed them to the bedroom Kenna had gone into last night. When he stepped into the room, Addy nodded to him from a chair in the corner. Kenna sat on the edge of the bed, holding her father's hand. Her mother was on the other side of the bed, sitting with her back to the headboard, holding her husband's other hand. The doctor, he assumed, stood at the foot of the bed, his hands folded together.

He stepped further into the room and Kenna turned her head and smiled at him. She held her hand out to him and he closed the distance between them. Her hand was small and cold. He held her tightly, offering silent support.

She turned to her dad. His eyes were closed, his breathing was labored, and uneven, his mouth hung open. "Daddy, he's here. The boy I told you about. Spencer."

Niya opened her eyes and smiled gently at him. He saw her squeeze her husband's hand.

Spencer kneeled on one knee next to Kenna and wrapped his arm around her back, holding her as close as he could. Her hand slid across his shoulders and stopped at the back of his head, her fingers winding into his hair at his nape.

"Daddy, this is Spencer."

"Hello, Mr. Lawrence. It's nice to meet you."

His eyes fluttered slightly. Recognition? Maybe a stranger in the room bothered him.

The door opened once again, and a man with dark hair and green eyes stepped into the room. Niya sobbed, and the man moved to her side of the bed and bent down to hug her.

"Howie, Jonnie's here." Niya scooted off the bed, and

Jonnie sat next to Howie. He leaned over and chucked Kenna on the shoulder. She smiled. "Jon, this is Spencer. Spencer, my youngest brother, and pain in the butt, Jon."

Spencer nodded as Jon looked down at his father and softly ran his fingers down his father's face. "Dad, I love you."

Kenna's sniffles reached his ears, and he squeezed her closer. She laid her head next to his, their temples touching. Silent tears slid down his face as he watched this stoic family say goodbye to their patriarch. He hoped when the day came, he could be as good at saying goodbye as this family. It was a lesson everyone should learn.

They'd sat quietly for another twenty minutes when Howie's breathing stuttered. The doctor sat on the bed behind Kenna and reached forward with his stethoscope and listened for a few quiet moments.

He wordlessly pulled his stethoscope back and rested it around his neck. He stood quietly and nodded to Niya.

She smiled sadly and took Howie's hand in hers once again. The two siblings and their mother surrounded him, while Addy, he and the doctor stood back in the room. They all watched as Howie gained his angel wings and left his earthly body for life in heaven.

Afterwards, Kenna leaned forward and kissed her father on the cheek, then stood and wrapped her arms around Spencer's waist. It was a connection he needed more than anything right now. He wanted to be here with her at this moment, but truth be told, he needed Kenna to be here with him. He'd seen his fellow servicemen pass in his day. It was always gut-wrenching and solemn, but it was usually much faster, like ripping off a Band-Aid. He'd never sat vigil as one passed, and it was a unique experience for sure.

Kenna turned and hugged Addy. "Thank you for being here, Addy."

Addy smiled serenely. "I'm happy to be here to support you all."

Kenna turned to him again and held him close. Addy stepped out of the room and he waited until Kenna was ready before taking her hand and leading her out to the living room.

He sat in the chair he'd occupied last night and Kenna snuggled on his lap. His arms wrapped around her, her head on his shoulder. He glanced out the window and saw Addy outside on the phone. He assumed she was calling the HOG or her parents. Likely her parents. All he wanted to do right now was call his parents and tell them he loved and missed them.

About an hour later, Helissa showed up at the house with Lara, carrying food containers and cookies. They set a spread up on the counter and everyone ate together. He formally met Jonathon and learned about his life in Florida.

The coroner came and left with Howie. Later in the evening, Kenna's brother Sean made it home.

His burner phone buzzed, and he read a text from Tate.

> "You got another text with a picture of the
> Lawrence home."

Whoever it was knew they were here. Or at least, knew Kenna was here.

36

She awoke as the sun streamed in through the window. The large, warm body she'd grown to expect behind her wasn't there. Rolling over, the dent in Spencer's pillow remained, but Spencer had gotten up and quietly left the room.

She looked at the clock on the bedside table. It was eight-thirty. She hadn't slept this late since she'd been a teenager.

As she stood in the shower, she envisioned the warm water washing yesterday's sadness away. After stepping out of the shower, she realized it didn't. Her heart hurt. Her dad would no longer be around to answer questions or offer advice, and she wondered how she'd get through the rest of her life. It seemed empty in a way she'd never experienced.

After dressing, she left the sanctuary of the bedroom she shared with Spencer and felt a vulnerability she'd never felt before.

People filled the kitchen. Spencer's teammates, Lara

and Helissa, they were all there. Spencer smiled at her. "Good morning."

"Morning."

Lara wrapped her in a warm embrace. "Good morning. I'm here if you need anything."

"Thank you. I don't even know what I need to be honest."

Lara nodded. "I know. Remember, only last year I went through this."

Kenna's eyes rounded. "Oh, God, I'm so sorry. I completely forgot Lara. I guess I'm all wrapped up in my sadness. Please forgive me."

Lara shook her pretty head and locked eyes with her. "No need to be sorry. For me, besides the grief of knowing I'd never see him again, I had things to deal with emotionally. The betrayals, lies, Kent. So much stuff to unpack, and it takes time. I'm still unpacking things."

"I bet you are." She took a deep breath. "I have stuff too, you know. To unpack. Colt, and Daddy's decisions to not have him arrested. I felt that betrayal and we never talked about it. Now I never can."

"Yeah. That's the unpacking part. It'll hit you in waves. You'll be angry. Sad. Hurt. And feel like there's no way to sort it or settle it because he's gone. But I offer you my support. We can unpack together."

"Lara. Thank you."

Lara squeezed her in a hug once more, then stepped away.

Spencer hugged her close and kissed the top of her head. "We've eaten, but Helissa saved you a plate. Sit down and I'll get it for you."

She took her usual seat at the table. Maya reached

across and grabbed her hand. "We're all here for you if you need anything."

She smiled. A bit surprised the tears weren't falling down her cheeks, but she'd cried so much yesterday there weren't more tears. Myles, Henry, Addy, and Tate all nodded their heads in agreement.

"Thank you all so much. I promise to ask if I need anything."

Spencer set a plate in front of her and a cup of coffee. It smelled so good and her stomach rumbled slightly.

She began eating as Tate spoke. "So, Kenna, we were just discussing the texts yesterday and the email."

"You mean the day before yesterday?" She sipped her coffee.

Spencer cleared his throat slightly. "We received another text yesterday, Kenna."

Her head swiveled slowly to look into his eyes. "What did it say?"

He frowned slightly, his handsome face still handsome. "Nothing. It was a picture of your parents' house."

Her brows shot up. "He was there?"

"Someone was."

"When?"

Spencer's eyes didn't leave hers. When he replied, his tone was even and sure and it gave her some comfort. "Addy's car is in the driveway in the picture. But the doctor's car isn't yet. So, after you and Addy arrived but before he did."

She turned to Addy. Addy nodded. "I was watching as we drove and didn't see anyone following us. But, if it's Colt, he'd likely know the direction we were going and drive past later to see if his hunch was correct."

She whispered, "Yeah."

Tate continued. "The picture you received in your text was of you after you'd been beaten. The direction of the picture suggests it was taken from somewhere near the law office next door, Smith Squared."

"I would have seen someone. I don't know how that could be."

Spencer softly rubbed her back, and she set her fork on her plate quietly. Her heart beat so fast it hurt. Her throat dried up, and she felt slightly dizzy.

Spencer softly said, "The picture I received of you walking into Lara's Delights seems to have been taken from the County Road, or someone on the end of the BRR road, just off the county road."

Her hands began shaking, so she held them together in her lap. "I don't remember seeing anyone pass on the road as I walked in, but I wouldn't think of that as being unusual, so I wouldn't have paid attention. I heard nothing like Colt's loud pipes. That would have caught my attention."

Spencer and Tate both nodded.

Myles said, "With cameras so good now, pictures can be taken from a great distance and still be clear. We're running some diagnostics on the photos now to see what type of camera they were taken on. Usually there's meta-data in photographs that are captured with date, time, location, camera type, make, model and, if it's a cellphone, even the owner's name. But we're recapturing these pictures after deletion and they've been manipulated, so not all the data is readily available."

Spencer still had his hand on her back. "For today, I don't know what has to be done to make arrangements for your father, but I'll be with you everywhere you go."

"Don't you have to work?"

His brows rose. "This is my work today. And tomorrow. And every day until we find out who's sending these texts and ensure your complete safety."

37

Standen listened as the phone rang. His stomach clenched with each ring that went unanswered. Finally, his mom picked up the phone. "Hi, honey. How are you doing?"

Relief swept through his body at the sound of her voice. "I'm good. I've called twice but didn't get through. I was beginning to worry."

His mom's laugh filled his heart with joy. "I'm sorry. Your dad and I are staying at Hawk and Roxanne's cabin, and the reception out there is terrible."

"How are they all doing?"

Her voice was light and happy when she responded. "They're great. They've done so much work on the cabin and he's beginning to talk retirement."

"Wow. Now that's something."

"Tell me what's going on with you, honey."

He closed his eyes and pictured his mom, her reddish hair in curls around her face. Her sweet nature always filled him with love. "I met a girl." He swallowed the knot in his throat. Saying it out loud to his mom was something he'd never done before. Not someone this special, anyway.

"Oh, hang on, I'm sitting down next to your dad so you can tell us both about her."

He heard the rustle of her clothing, then a squeak as she sat on the sofa in the living room. He could see the exact spot where she sat. He heard her whisper, "Spencer met a girl."

"Hey, Spence. Tell us all about this girl you met," his dad said.

"Hi, Dad." He swallowed and took a deep breath. "I met her quite by accident. The accident being I was jogging and not paying attention and I literally ran into her."

His parents laughed.

"We later met at the construction office where I found out she's a process server. Her dad owns the business, and she'd left town years ago, but came back because her dad was sick and needed help."

His mom, always sweet and caring, replied, "Oh, I hope her dad is alright."

He swallowed the sadness that settled in his throat. "He passed yesterday. I was there with her and the family."

His mom's sadness made him tear up. "Oh, honey. I'm so sorry. For you and her."

He breathed in deeply a few times and squeezed his eyes shut. "I'm so happy to hear your voices."

His dad's firm voice replied, "Spencer, we're always happy to hear your voice too. We love you so much. We're incredibly proud of you."

Sobs broke from his chest and he gripped his phone

tightly. They all sat together in silence for a few moments. His voice cracked when he replied, "Watching Kenna's dad pass yesterday made me realize a few things. How much I love both of you and Dani. I miss you all."

He heard them both choke back tears. His mom managed a response first. "We miss you too. Why don't we plan to come down and visit? We'd like to meet Kenna."

"We'd like that very much. I want you to meet her. She's...special."

"Where is she now?" his mom asked.

He took in a few breaths, finally able to let go of the sadness and loneliness for his family. "She's getting ready. We're heading to her parents' house this morning to make arrangements."

His dad's voice cleared. "I'm proud of you for being there for her, Spence."

"Well, that's the other thing. She's being stalked. Read the reports Tate uploaded this morning. I'm doing everything in my power to protect her, but we're trying to find the asshole, so we know she's safe."

"I'll read them as soon as we hang up," his dad responded.

His mom replied, "I'll plan today to be there soon."

"It's likely we'll have Mr. Lawrence's funeral on Saturday."

"Then we'll be there for support. I'll talk to Lara about a room for us to sleep in."

"We have all the room you need. I can't wait to see you both."

Their call ended after the love yous and he inhaled a deep breath and let it whoosh out. He'd needed that. He swiped at his eyes, clearing the remaining moisture from the tears he'd shed, ran his hand down his face and stood from the picnic table he'd been sitting on.

"Hey, is everything alright?" Kenna asked from behind him.

He turned, "Yeah. I just needed to talk to my parents."

"Oh," she whispered.

"After watching you lose your father yesterday, I needed to speak to my parents. I called them twice last night, and they didn't answer, so of course, after what you went through, I assumed the worst."

Kenna moved toward him and wrapped her arms around his waist. She squeezed him tight and laid her head on his chest. "I get that."

He swallowed. "Anyway, they're good and they'll be here in two days to visit. They're excited to meet you."

"Daddy's funeral might be Saturday."

"And they'll be here for support. Their words, not mine."

"Oh, such a sad day to meet them." Kenna said into his chest.

"But, after this, I don't want to wait any longer for them to meet you." Her beautiful face turned up to look into his, and he kissed her lips. "I don't want to wait another day. I love you, Kenna Lawrence."

Tears welled, then spilled from her perfect green eyes. He wiped them away gently with his fingers and she said, "I love you, Spencer Lawson. I love you."

He kissed her again, this time sealing the expression of love they'd each offered the other. He knew he loved her when they'd argued a few days ago. It hit him like a sledgehammer when he'd left for work in the morning without a kind word. He'd felt terrible all day, and he vowed to himself then he'd never leave the house again without telling her to have a great day or a kind word. And now, he'd never leave the house without telling her he loved her. That would be their new morning routine. It felt good. It felt right.

38

The soft murmuring of her mom's voice and her brother's responses circled around her, but Kenna was focused on other things. Spencer, first. He stood in the living room, just off the kitchen, his broad, strong back to her as he stared out the window. His hands were in his front pockets, but he wasn't relaxed at all. He tried looking casual for her; she was sure of it. But he was worried about the texts and email. He was thinking about his parents. And likely, he was worried about her plans.

And that was the elephant in the room right now. What were her plans? On the one hand, she had a ready-made business here. Process service was something she'd done since she was eighteen. Years before she could legally serve documents, she'd ridden along with her dad and kept all the records.

When she moved to Houston, she'd done the same thing. But she'd worked for another agency. Something there told her she wouldn't stay. But she honestly never thought she'd come back here to Glen Hollow.

"Kenna?"

She turned to face her mom. "Sorry mom, I didn't hear you."

"I asked you if you'd take care of ordering the flowers for your father."

Spencer turned to face her. She swallowed. Her eyes landed on his for a moment, then back to her mom. "Of course."

Spencer's jaw tightened. The muscle in his jaw moved. She smiled his way, and he nodded in return before sitting in the chair near the window.

Her phone rang, and she looked at the number. Not recognizing it, she answered, "The Paper Trail."

"Kenna is that you? This is Peter Murphy. I just heard about Howie's passing. I'm very sorry for your loss."

"Thank you, Mr. Murphy." She stood and walked away from the table and the chattering about arrangements, down the hallway toward her old bedroom. She pushed the door open, and it was like stepping back in time. Her twin bed still dominated the middle of the room. The same pink and yellow floral bedspread she'd had in high school still draped over the bed. Her little wooden desk was freshly polished and held pictures of her in her high school years. Cheerleading pictures, her graduation photo. Friends and various activities she'd taken part in during her high school years.

She sat at the foot of the bed, staring at the pictures of years gone by.

Murphy continued. "I have some papers that need to be served in the next couple of weeks. Are you taking on Howie's business like the good ole' days?"

"I am. At least for right now, I'm here working in the office."

"Good. I'll have the documents couriered over to you this afternoon."

"I'll pick them up, if you don't mind. The office is closed today and tomorrow. The funeral will be Saturday, and next Monday the office will reopen."

Mr. Murphy sighed. "How about this? Let me have them brought to your office on Monday. I get wrapped up with business and forget the small things. It's something Mrs. Murphy complains about all the time. Again, we'll miss Howie. He was a special man."

She smiled. "Thank you. He was for sure."

A sound caught her attention, and she turned toward the door to see Spencer's gigantic frame leaning against the doorjamb.

"Hi," she whispered.

"Hi. Business doesn't stop, even when life does. Does it?"

She shook her head and swallowed. Spencer stepped into the room and made the room impossibly small. He stared at the photos on her desk, a soft grin forming on his lips as he picked up a picture of her in her cheerleading uniform.

He teased, "Hubba-hubba."

She shook her head and giggled. "Hardly."

"Honey, you were a beautiful young lady in high school and you're a beautiful woman now. The first time I saw you, I thought you were stunning."

"Hardly. You ran me over."

"Ah, but I saved you from falling on your ass. It was me who took the brunt of that fall."

She grinned as he grimaced, rotating his shoulder. "Oh, were you seriously injured?" she giggled. She ran her hand over his firm shoulder, then let her hand slide down his chest.

"Yes, I was." He kissed the tip of her nose. "You stole my heart that day."

"Did I now?" She kissed his chin, then wrapped her arms around his waist. Tilting her head up to look into his handsome face, she smiled. "You aren't feeding me full of your sad pickup lines now, are you?"

"Sweetheart, I don't have sad pickup lines."

She laughed, and his chest rumbled in laughter with her. He kissed her lips then looked into her eyes. "Is everything alright?"

"Yes. Attorney Murphy needs some papers served, but he'll have them brought to the office on Monday."

"Okay."

"Now, though, I guess I have to go to Bloomin' Lovely and order flowers for daddy's funeral."

"Can't you order them by phone?"

She sighed. "I can. But I need to get out of here. It's so glum and depressing and I have so much on my mind with everything else. I just need a break. Do you mind taking a drive after we order flowers?"

He kissed her lips once again, and she closed her eyes, enjoying the feel of their lips together. They were a perfect fit. His were full and soft and they always molded to hers perfectly.

His solid body, pressed to hers, made her feel secure. His powerful arms around her made her feel safe. The aroma of his aftershave surrounding her made her body feel many fun things. She loved this man and life was moving fast.

His chest rose and fell and when he responded, the

vibrations as he spoke gave her goosebumps. "We can take a ride. I can ask Helissa to pack a picnic lunch and we can go somewhere alone, just the two of us."

She shivered. "That sounds perfect."

39

They picked the flowers, procured a picnic basket, grabbed a blanket, and now they were driving out of town toward Brookwood.

Spencer watched the signs as they traveled down the county road and out of Glen Hollow. The sun shone high in the sky; the weather was now in the high seventies and the horses they passed played and frolicked and loved the weather as much as he did.

K[illegible] a young colt ran behind its mother. She turned her head to see if he saw it too, and their eyes locked. His heart kicked up about four notches as he stared at the dark-haired beauty with the soulful green eyes.

He reached over the console and she laid her hand in his. He lifted her hand to his lips and kissed her fingers.

Tossing her long dark hair over her shoulder, she slid a saucy gaze his way. "Where are you taking me, handsome?"

He grinned and winked. "I have some connections. And those connections have secret hideaways. I'm taking you to a secret hideaway for the afternoon. We'll be safe and alone. We'll be able to sit and talk or just sit and enjoy nature."

"You'd be fine sitting and enjoying nature and not talking?"

He smiled at her remark. "Kenna, I know we haven't known each other long enough to know lots of things about each other, but I can sit for long hours doing nothing. When I'm with you, just being with you is enough. If you don't feel like talking, I understand. I only want to be with you while you process the things in your head. And I'll make sure you're safe while you think about the things you need to get straight."

She stared at him for a long time. He had to keep checking the road to make sure he didn't run them off it and cause an accident. But every time his eyes slid to hers, she was watching him.

"Thank you." Her smile was genuine and more beautiful every time he saw it.

He pulled onto a dirt road marked only by a fire marker and a mailbox, leaning to the right so far he wondered at the last time the mail had actually been delivered there.

The road curved right and left, and there were rocks jutting from the dirt in various places. Finally, more than a mile from the main road, a clearing formed in the trees and a small cabin stood, straight and neat and proud. There were rocking chairs and a glider rocker for two on the wrap-around porch.

"Oh, wow. That's charming," she breathed.

He chuckled. "Let's go see the inside."

He hurried around the truck to help her down, stealing a kiss as he did. He reached into the backseat and pulled out the picnic basket Helissa had made them and the blanket. Taking Kenna's hand in his, he walked them to the front of the cottage. Once on the front of the porch, he could see a pond and a mama duck with her five ducklings lazily floating the day away. He pointed to them and Kenna laughed.

"Oh, those are adorable."

They watched the ducks for a bit then he turned the key in the lock on the cottage and ushered Kenna inside.

"Oh, Spencer, this is adorable." She declared.

He nodded. It was nice inside. Clean white walls and decorated in the style of a lake home. The living room and kitchen were open to each other; a short hallway led from the living room to a bathroom and two small bedrooms.

"Who owns this cottage?" she asked.

"Baxter's brother. He lives in Tennessee now, and it sits empty mostly. I asked Baxter if he had a place we could go that would be private, so you could clear your head. He eagerly offered this place."

"Wow. Thank you. Please tell him thank you."

He chuckled, "I did, but I'll send your thanks as well."

Kenna looked around the cottage and checked the view from each window before asking. "So, what now?"

He chuckled again. "What do you want to do?"

"Honestly? Do you mind if we just sit out on the porch for a bit?"

"I don't mind at all."

He opened the door for her and smiled when she selected the glider for two and sat down, patting the place beside her.

He sat next to her and put his arm around her shoulders. Her head tilted and rested on his shoulder. He moved the glider back and forth. Slow and steady. The weather was perfect under the roof of the porch. The songs of the birds and the movement of the ducks on the pond lent itself to peace and tranquility.

They rocked for a long time. His eyes grew heavy and his head bobbed a couple of times. It was so peaceful here. He tried remembering the last time he'd felt so comfortable with another person. Sitting and saying nothing felt—right. The only other person in his life he'd ever sat with and not talked to was his mom. She seemed to sense when he needed calm, and she was always there as he grew up to give him that. Now Kenna.

"This is nice," she whispered.

"MmmHmm."

He continued moving them evenly. Kenna inhaled a deep breath and let it out slowly. Then she lifted her head and sat up straight.

"You know, I've got some big decisions to make right now."

He shifted on the loveseat. "I'm aware."

"How do you feel about that?"

He chuckled. "I don't see that they're my decisions to make, honey."

She nodded, her eyes on the ducks. "But they affect you."

"Yes. I'm painfully aware of that fact."

She turned and looked into his eyes then. She slightly bunched her brows and pronounced the worry line between them. "What do you want?"

"Nope. I'm not deciding for you, Kenna." He leaned forward with his elbows on his knees.

She shifted so her body faced his. Their rocking movement stopped. "Spencer. I love you. I honest-to-goodness love you. No one in my life has ever made me feel like you do. These past weeks have been scary, and sweet, and amazing, and sad. So many things, but the one constant is you."

He leaned back and placed his elbow on the back of the seat. His fingers slipped into the dark, silky hair that fell over her shoulder. He watched the satiny strands flow through his fingers like water and fall back onto her shoulder.

"Honey. I love you like I've never loved anyone else before. That said, I don't want to lose you. I want us to have a real chance to see how we fit for the long term. But I know you don't feel safe here, for obvious reasons. And, as much as I'll do anything in my power to make sure you're always safe, there will be one day when I'm not around. There is also the chance we could move somewhere else. Indiana is where my job is. We could go there."

"Right." She licked her lips.

He continued. "I can't make your decisions for you because you need to sort them for yourself. In the end, you need to know the decisions you make are yours and only yours. I'd never want you to regret staying or going because I suggested it."

40

He had something beautiful for sure. Did she understand? She did, but it left her shoulders with all the weight on them for now. She was a big girl though, and she'd make the decisions she knew she could live with. She smiled as she thought, that's exactly what he meant for her to do.

She watched the ducks waddle out of the pond and up on the grass. They shook their bodies, ruffled their feathers, and picked at the ground looking for food. Spencer's stomach growled, and she turned to him. "Let's go inside and eat."

His grin was beautiful. "I thought you'd never ask."

He stood and held his hand out to her. She laid her hand in his and enjoyed the connection, just that created.

Inside the cottage, he led her to a chair at the table and opened the picnic basket. He pulled out a bottle of wine, two stemless wine glasses, and an opener. He laid cheese, sliced and arranged prettily on a plate on the table. A loaf of French bread, sliced and repackaged, a container with cold cuts arranged in a circle, and a container with lettuce and small jars of mustard, mayonnaise, and ranch dressing followed. Finally, a container with fresh vegetables. He set the basket aside and began opening the wine while she arranged the rest of the food on the table.

"Wow, when you ask Helissa for a picnic, she delivers," she exclaimed.

"She is a great addition to our group. She's dependable, she doesn't ask questions, and she does a great job keeping us full and clean."

She laughed. "That she does."

Spencer poured them each a glass of wine and sat across the table from her. It was a small round wooden table, so they were still very close. He held up his glass of wine. "Here's to us, Kenna. And to you and all the decisions you have to make."

She smiled. "Here's to us." The other would come. Hopefully.

They tapped their glasses together and sipped their wine. Spencer's stomach growled again, and she giggled.

"Eat. Hurry before your stomach revolts."

He laughed but began building a sandwich. She did the same.

"What are your parents like?" she asked.

His grin was lopsided, as he had food in his mouth. He swallowed, then responded, "They're great. My dad has been an operative for over thirty years now. My mom stayed home with me when I was younger and she helped homeschool my teammates and me. We all grew up together and the moms and dads took part in our education."

"So you didn't go to public school?"

"No, they considered it too dangerous. Some missions

our parents went on brought criminals too close for comfort. My half-sister, Dani, was kidnapped once when Maya and Myles' mom was guarding her. My mom and dad were just beginning their relationship and my mom let herself be kidnapped so she could find Dani. From all accounts, my dad was a raging bull to get them back. So, to answer your question, they take safety seriously. They love us all, meaning my teammates and also Dani and me, without exception. They are supportive and their love is what I've always dreamed of finding for myself."

Hmm. She watched his face as he bit into his sandwich, but she kept replaying his comments in her head. "...their love is what I've always dreamed of finding for myself." His mom was brave and so was his dad. His teammates were too. They put themselves in danger to save others every day. Spencer didn't hesitate to help her. He didn't wait to be asked, he just did. If she was to be the kind of partner he'd always dreamed of, she'd need to be the kind of woman his mom was. Brave.

She swallowed another bite of her sandwich and sipped her wine.

She received a text and her stomach nearly turned over as she read it.

"Have a nice time."

And the picture was of this cottage.

She swallowed the food in her mouth and took a deep breath. Turning her phone so Spencer could see it, she waited for his response.

He jumped up and looked out the windows, then he turned to her. "Lock the doors behind me. I'm going out to see if I can find him."

She jumped up and locked the doors, watching from window to window to see if she could see anyone lurking. She picked up her phone and looked at the picture again and determined the direction to be on the other side of the pond.

When she looked out the front windows, she saw Spencer heading in that direction, and she decided to help him find Colt. That's what Spencer's mom would do.

She took a deep breath and unlocked the front door. She stepped off the porch and followed Spencer's footsteps. Perhaps Colt would see her and react, which would ferret out his location. One could hope.

Her phone buzzed again, and she pulled up the picture that was attached to it. She whipped her head around to see if Colt was on the front porch, because that's definitely where the picture had been taken from. She headed toward the cottage to check if he had made his way inside. She listened closely for any movement or sound, but could only hear frogs and birds chirping and the buzz of bugs as she kicked them up from the grass.

The sun glinted off something on the north side of the cottage and she changed her direction. Her heart raced, and her palms dampened as she neared the area. She struggled to breathe evenly. She neared the north corner to the cottage and peered around the side to see if anyone was there.

She found herself pulled backwards, and a hand pressed over her mouth, muffling her screams. She wriggled and floundered, trying to pull away. Her heels struggled to dig in as she was dragged back toward a vehicle, and panic flooded her body that she'd be taken away from here without Spencer knowing.

41

He struggled to keep her upright. Damn, she was a fighter.

"Stop," he hissed near her ear.

He loosened his hold on her body but kept his hand tight over her mouth. "Kenna. It's me, Spencer. Stop fighting."

She went still to the point he worried she'd passed out.

"Nod if you recognize my voice."

Her head bobbed. So, so. He held her tightly to his chest.

"I'm going to let you go, but you can't run or scream, honey. Okay?"

He felt her slightly relax and her head moved again. He loosened his grip on her and removed his hand from her mouth.

The second she was free, she whirled around to face him, her eyes rounded in fear. Then, her brain registered it was him and he saw the relief as it washed over her face.

He held his forefinger over his lips and gently pulled her behind his body. The sound of a motor broke the silence of the area and he ran toward the sound. The long curvy dirt road into the cottage kept the vehicle out of his sight and he stopped running, knowing it was futile. He'd never catch a moving vehicle on foot. He jogged back to find Kenna standing where he'd left her, and he took her hand and pulled her into the cottage. Inside, he locked the door and turned to see her staring at him.

"What the hell was that?" he barked.

She flinched, then tears fell from her eyes. He let out a breath, just now realizing how scared he'd been seeing Kenna head toward the place he'd seen the arm of a person just seconds before. He took one step and reached out to pull her body into his. His heart still raced and his breathing was uneven, but he needed to feel her against him and he didn't like it when she cried. At all.

"Hey, it's okay," he murmured into her hair. His hands dug into the warm dark locks as her face laid against his chest. His fingers moved on her scalp, his body liked the feel of her soft curves against him.

She sniffed, and he pulled back to look into her eyes. "I asked you to stay here and lock the doors."

She sobbed then, and it hurt his heart. After a few moments, she spoke, though it was difficult to understand.

"I wanted to be brave. Like your mom."

He closed his eyes and held her closer. "I didn't mean..." He took a deep breath and directed her to the sofa with him. He sat down and pulled her onto his lap.

"I don't want you putting yourself in harm's way because my mom did. It wasn't what my dad wanted her to do, and he was pissed that she did. I was merely telling you that because you asked what they were like."

She sniffed. "But you said you wanted a love like theirs."

He put his hands on either side of her head and forced her to look into his eyes. "Because I do. But being reckless isn't love. What I want is how they treat each other. How they respect each other. How they love each other."

She sniffed again, and he glanced over to find a box of tissues on the little table next to the sofa. He pulled one free and handed it to her. He watched as she wiped her eyes, careful not to smear her makeup. Then she gently blew her nose. When she'd cleaned up, her beautiful green eyes landed on his and he smiled.

"My mom will be the first to tell you she'd been stupid. But she'd felt guilty because it was her former boyfriend who'd found her and chance put him in proximity to Dani, so he took her instead."

"Okay." She hiccupped for air and he continued to stare into her eyes.

"I'm the operative in this relationship. Deal?"

"Deal," she whispered.

He pulled her to his chest and wrapped his arms around her and her arms willingly came around his neck, locking them together. She pulled away, stood briefly, straddled his legs and sat on his lap again, their chests pushed together. He pulled her as close to him as he could and closed his eyes. Her silky dark hair fell around them, the fresh scent of it his new favorite smell.

After a while, Kenna pulled back to look at him. "I'm sorry." She swallowed, and he grinned.

"Thank you. Never do that again."

"I won't."

He huffed out a breath. "Now, what did you see?"

"Nothing. Oops..." She reached behind her and pulled her phone out and tapped. Turning the phone to him, she continued. "I got this text. It came from back here. When I turned to look, I saw the glint of something on the north side of the cottage, so I was going to see if Colt was there."

"Did you see him?"

Her head shook. "No." She swallowed. "Did you see him?"

"No. I saw an arm. Briefly. Likely taking the picture. And then I heard the vehicle leave."

"I didn't hear Colt's pipes."

"No, I didn't either. So, he was in an unfamiliar vehicle or it wasn't him."

She gasped. "Who else would want to scare me?"

He stared at her face, her beautiful face. The bruises were fading and without makeup, he could see them, but it was merely a discoloration at this point. He could see that she had concealed the bruising with makeup.

"Hopefully, we'll have an answer soon. But, I'd say for now, our peace and tranquility has been disturbed. Should we head back home?"

She nodded. "I'll call my mom on the way and see if there is anything else I should do today."

"Do you want to go back and spend time with your brothers?"

She blew out a breath and puffed her cheeks out. "I know this might sound bad, but no. Not today. They're all sad. I'm sad too, but I haven't told them what's been happening and my mind is so split on all of this. And I just can't sit in that sad house right now. It's clawing at my stomach."

He kissed her forehead and held her head in his hands once again. "Kenna. I love you. I want nothing to happen to you, ever. Please don't be a hero."

"I won't. I'll let you be my hero."

42

"Get some rest, honey. I'll see you in the morning."

Her mom sounded so sad, Kenna thought.

"I will. Good night, Mama. Call me if you need anything."

Spencer's phone rang as she hung up. She grinned, and he shook his head as he answered with the Bluetooth in his truck.

"Hi, Mom."

"Hi, Spencer. Your dad and I will be in later tonight. We're leaving here in a few minutes.

"That's great. Mom, Kenna is here with me. Kenna, meet my mom, Yvette."

"Hi, Yvette. It's nice to meet you."

She felt sheepish, but it was better than this long anticipation. Plus, she'd been through enough lately that pleasant surprises were few, so she'd take it.

"It's nice to meet you, Kenna. I'm looking forward to chatting with you when we get there."

"I'm looking forward to meeting you, too."

"Also, please accept our condolences on the passing of your father. We're deeply sorry."

She swallowed the lump in her throat and blinked away the tears. "Thank you."

She took some deep breaths and Spencer took her hand in his.

"We'll watch for you to pull in. We'll sit around the fire pit and have a friendly chat. How does that sound?"

His mom giggled. "It sounds like the best old times ever."

"Good. See you soon. Love you."

"Love you too, honey. See you soon."

Spencer tapped the button on his steering wheel to end the call, then sat back with a contemplative look on his face.

"So, will you tell me about the best old times?"

He laughed, and she stared at him. He was handsome always. But, when he laughed, whew, that was something.

"Growing up, we'd build a fire in our fire pit and sit around roasting marshmallows and having drinks and chatting. It was quiet time and therapeutic in that I'd tell them everything about my day. They'd tell me about theirs, and we were just a regular family. I loved it best when Dani was home. She's a spitfire and she's fun."

"Aww, that sounds like enjoyable times. I'm happy to be included in your best old times."

He chuckled. "It'll be the best new times now." He kissed her fingers again, and she swooned. Sort of. But wow!

He pulled into Paxton's Grocery. "Gotta go get marshmallows, graham crackers, and chocolate bars."

"Okay. I haven't had a s'more in...wow, I can't remember the last time."

"Then it's time to have one. Or two."

He strode around the truck to help her out, a ritual she'd grown to love. They walked into Paxton's hand in hand, and she realized it was the most normal moment she'd had in weeks. That was sad.

Spencer pushed a cart and stopped in front of the marshmallows. He dropped three large bags of them into the cart and her mouth dropped open.

"Holy crap. How many are you going to eat?"

"Honey, I have teammates at home who have good appetites."

"Okay." She followed along as he picked three boxes of graham crackers from a shelf and the same with the chocolate bars. He found three eight-packs of full-size chocolate bars. She almost got a cavity from the sweets in the cart.

He swung by the liquor aisle and bought four cases of beer and two cases of hard seltzers.

"We're really having a party tonight," she teased.

"It's so overdue."

She followed along as he browsed the store for anything else that looked good.

"Hi, Kenna, is that you?"

Kenna blinked then realized who had addressed her. "Hi, Ami. Yes, it's me."

Spencer shifted alongside her and she slightly shook her head and tried to not look around in case Colt had come to the store with Ami. "This is Spencer Lawson. Spencer, this is Ami Pearson. She's engaged to Colt."

Spencer reached out to shake Ami's hand. Ami was staring at her and didn't notice for a moment. Kenna ignored the tiny prickles at the back of her neck.

"Nice to meet you, Ami."

The smile didn't reach her eyes, but she replied. "Uh. Oh. It's nice to meet you too."

Ami took a deep breath. "Are you staying in town long, Kenna?"

Kenna looked up at Spencer, and the grin he returned made her heartbeat speed up. He did that.

"I'm not sure right now."

Spencer interrupted the conversation. "Hey, it was nice to meet you Ami, but we have to get going. My parents are coming into town tonight."

Ami jerked at the abrupt change but nodded. "Oh. Of course. Have fun."

Spencer placed his hand at the small of her back and ushered them quickly to the checkout.

After loading the groceries into the truck, they headed toward the HOG. She glanced at the clock on the console and saw it was six p.m. Where had the day gone?

"How long have you known Ami?" Spencer asked.

She shrugged. "You know it's a small town. I've known her since school, back in the day. Obviously, I didn't stay in contact while I was gone."

"Okay." He turned into the garage. She relaxed as he shut off the truck. It felt like home here.

After carrying the groceries into the kitchen, Spencer glanced at her. "Can I have your phone?"

Her brows furrowed, then smoothed, and she handed over her phone. He held it high and nodded at Tate, who was eating dinner with Lara and Myles.

"Kenna received two more texts today."

Tate shook his head. "Plug it in. I'll check it when I'm finished."

"Will do. And my parents will be here in a couple of hours. We're having a fire in the pit and making s'mores."

Lara laughed. "I wondered what you were doing with all that stuff."

Kenna nodded at Lara. "It's daunting. My teeth hurt looking at all this sugar."

Lara nodded. "Dinner is in the oven, staying warm. Help yourself."

She pulled plates from the cupboard and pulled a roast with the fixings from the oven. Filling Spencer's plate and half-filling hers, she carried them to the table and sat.

Lara smiled at her. "Did you get everything planned today for your dad's funeral?"

"They did. I only ordered the flowers, then Spence and I went for a drive. That's when I got the texts."

Tate glanced her way. "We'll find out who's doing it, Kenna. Cyber Unit at RAPTOR told me this afternoon they're close to pinpointing the IP address."

"That will be a joyous day."

Spencer came back into the kitchen and sat at the table with them. He tackled his food and she watched in amazement. Where did he put it all?

Addy entered the kitchen from the living area. "I hear we're having guests tonight?"

Myles nodded. "I guess we're partying too." He nodded to the pile of marshmallows, chocolate, and crackers on the counter.

"Oh, my God. That's a lot of sugar."

Spencer laughed. "You should see all the beer in my truck."

Myles laughed and stood with his plate. "I'll bring it in."

Henry entered the kitchen and sat at the table with them. He said nothing, but she'd noticed he didn't chat needlessly. Finally, Maya came into the room and stopped when she saw the pile of sugar on the counter. "What the hell?"

"The Lawsons will be here soon. Fire pit and drinking with s'mores tonight." Myles grinned as he set two cases of beer on the counter.

"Holy shit." Maya breathed.

Kenna sat back and watched these people chat, laugh, and live, and she realized why she enjoyed living here. They were awesome together. They were siblings with different parents. Except for Maya and Myles. It was comfortable here, and she felt safe in their presence. But what she really loved was Spencer. He'd been with her through so much.

He tossed another log on the fire and sat back in his chair. He reached for Kenna's hand and their fingers instantly locked. His dad glanced at him and nodded. He still wore that big ole beard to cover the scar on the side of his face. It bothered him more than anyone, and Spencer had never known his father without it. But his mom liked the beard and called Dad a lumberjack, which he said he didn't like, but secretly did.

Tate returned from the kitchen with a bucket full of beers and handed it around so everyone had a fresh drink.

His mom stood. "I'm heading to bed, folks. It's been a long day, but I look forward to spending the day with you tomorrow."

She stooped and kissed his cheek. "Love you, Spence." She winked at Kenna. "Night, honey." Soon, Kenna and the other team members went to bed, and the only ones left were his dad, Tate, and himself.

Tate scooted his chair closer and said, "Cyber has an IP. It's here in town, but it isn't Colt's address."

"They're sending me the physical address of the IP location in the morning. There were a couple more tests they wanted to run on it. They thought it was a business in town."

"I thought we ruled out Kent."

"We did. I don't think it's Kent's address either. They would have said something. They know of our suspicions."

His dad nodded. "I want to go with you when you find out who it is."

Spencer chuckled. "Aren't you on vacation or something?"

"I'm never on vacation when it concerns you or Dani, Spence."

He stared into his dad's eyes and nodded. "Thanks, Dad."

His dad nodded, tipped his beer bottle and finished it, then stood and said, "Night, boys."

Spencer leaned back in his chair and so did Tate. They rarely had time to chat like this anymore.

"Did you know you loved Lara right away?"

"Yep. I didn't admit it to myself right away, though. I thought she was interested in you."

He scoffed and drank down more of his beer. "She had eyes for you right away."

Tate shrugged but said nothing.

"Are you happy?" He turned to look at his friend. "I mean, are you happily married and happy you married when you did?"

"Yes, to both. We'd like to have kids. We're in our thirties and would like to start a family. I knew she was the one when I finally admitted it to myself. I didn't see why we needed to wait."

Spencer nodded. "Yeah."

They sat in silence for a long time. Tate finally broke it. "Are you thinking about marriage?"

He turned his head and looked his friend in the eye. "She needs to decide if she's staying here first. I don't want to muddy that water. If I ask her to stay and she does, then in a few years, if she's sorry and wants to leave, it will be because she wanted to make me happy. Not because she really wanted to be here."

"Makes sense. Doesn't make it easy, though."

"Nope." Spencer finished his beer. "I'm off to bed. Tomorrow is Howie's funeral planning and my parents are here. I should get some sleep."

"Sounds good. I'll let you know as soon as Cyber gets back to me in the morning."

"Thanks."

He used the poker and moved the logs around and Tate found the jug of water to douse the fire. They stood in silence, watching it for a moment, then they turned quietly and entered the HOG. As they parted to go to their respective rooms, they waved, but said nothing. The house was quiet. Neither wanted to break that.

He slid into the room where Kenna slept and stepped across to the bathroom. Closing the door, he stripped his smoky smelling clothes off and jumped into the shower. Padding quietly to the bed, naked as the day he was born, he slid between the covers and snuggled Kenna's naked body to his.

She rolled in his arms, her generous breasts pushed against his chest, and his cock came to life. She had that effect on him.

She giggled and her hand slid down his body and wrapped around his firm cock, pumping him slowly. Her lips kissed across his chest, he pushed into her hand firmly.

He was eager, not interested in foreplay. Sometimes it went that way. "I'm ready, honey."

She giggled low in her belly. "Me too."

He pushed her to her back and settled between her legs. "Fast. Yeah?"

"Yeah."

Her legs wrapped around his ass, and he slid into her and eagerly moved in and out. She met him thrust for thrust, just as excited for her release as he was for his.

His skin heated, but so did hers. The glow of her eyes in the dim moonlight mesmerized him as he slid into her warmth repeatedly. When he could hold back no longer, he shook his head. "Babe."

"Yeah," she whispered, and he let himself release into her warm, smooth body. She wasn't quite finished and pushed him onto his back, and ground against him a few times until her release washed over her. He loved it. Her sexy breasts glowed in the moonlight, the rest of her body shaded, and she looked like an ethereal siren beckoning him to do naughty things to her. Which he'd happily oblige.

She looked into his eyes, a slow smile crawled across her face. "I've never done that before."

He squeezed her hips between his hands then trailed them up to cradle her breasts. "Feel free to do it anytime you like. You're mesmerizing to watch."

Kenna walked along the rows of caskets in the funeral home's basement. Her mom sat in a chair, quietly crying, and she and her brothers tried to decide. How did you make that decision? You don't look for comfort.

Sean stopped in front of a casket that had a blue lining and hunting motifs detailing the outside.

"Dad liked blue." Sean said.

"He wasn't much of a hunter though," Kenna replied.

They moved on. Finally, Jonathon stopped at the end of a row and waited for them to catch up.

"I know Mom hasn't said and Dad didn't make the arrangements, but can we at least agree to not spend too much? Even at the low end of the spectrum, these caskets cost around three thousand dollars. It isn't like he's going to rest in peace better in a six-thousand-dollar casket and Mom might need the money one day."

Her brother Jonathon resembled her mom more than Sean or her. He had the blue eyes and sandy hair while she and Sean were dark-haired and green-eyed.

"I agree with that, Jon," she replied.

Jon glanced at Sean. "I agree."

Jon continued walking to the back of the room. "Okay, this casket is nice. It's pine, has a blue liner, and the outside isn't detailed in depth, but it's nice. It's only for the funeral home and the service. After that, no one will ever see it again."

She turned her head and glanced at Spencer, who dutifully stood near her mom. But his eyes never looked away from her. He nodded slightly, and she smiled softly in return.

"This makes sense," she agreed.

Sean turned his sad eyes toward her. She hadn't seen him smile since he'd gotten home. But, he was the baby of the family and had spent the most time with their father. "Do you think this will make our family look cheap to the townspeople?"

She slid her arm through Sean's and squeezed. "Sean. Why do we always have to care what the townspeople think of us?"

"Because of the business."

She inhaled through her nose and stared at the casket as Jon went to find the mortician.

"The business offers reliable, efficient service at a fair price. It always has and it always will."

"So, you're going to keep running The Paper Trail?"

She froze, her brows pushed together as she fixated on the blue liner in the casket before her. That business was as much a part of her as her father. It was where the two of them had spent the most time with each other. They shared humorous stories about one service or another, like when a man tried to avoid service by jumping on his tractor and flipping her father off on his low-speed escape. There were so many stories from years and years in the business.

"I'm not entirely sure yet." Her eyes darted to Spencer's ever-watchful gaze. Spencer was here, too. If they could get Colt to leave her alone, it would be idyllic. She could keep her family's business going, live with the sexiest man she'd ever laid eyes on, and maybe they'd get married and have babies. Beautiful, dark-haired, green-eyed babies.

"You'd better decide sooner rather than later." Sean nudged her. His eyes also landed on Spencer, who was watching them closely.

"I know," she whispered. Her heart felt heavier now. Like the weight of a thousand anchors landing on her shoulders. Her mom was here too. She'd be here to help with babies. She could raise her children to keep the business rolling along when she parted with this world. They could serve generations of families.

What if one day Spencer was transferred? He'd been transferred here to work. Who's to say he wouldn't be transferred somewhere else? Would she be expected to go with him?

Jonathon came back to them. "We're all set. The mortician is taking care of it all."

Sean nodded. "Thanks Jon. I guess we're all set then."

She inhaled deeply. "I guess."

Sean started walking to their mother, her arm still wrapped around his. She looked into Spencer's eyes as they neared, and she wondered how much he could hear. It was terribly quiet in this room. It made it even more depressing than it was. Which was saying a lot.

Jon helped their mom stand up. "We're all set, Mom.

They'll take care of everything from here. All we need to do is rest today. Tomorrow will be hard enough."

Slowly, her mom turned and held on to Jon's arm and they proceeded up the stairs. Sean followed behind them. Spencer wrapped his arm around her shoulders and kissed the top of her head. "Ready?"

"Yeah. Let's get out of here. It's creepy."

"Agreed."

As they ascended the stairs, her mind floated around so many topics, she almost felt dizzy. What she wouldn't give for some rest. But...

Spencer helped her into the truck and jumped in behind the wheel. "Where to?"

She frowned slightly. "My mom's. I guess neighbors and church friends have been dropping by nonstop and bringing food and drinks. We need to be there to help her out."

"Will do."

He put the truck into drive and onto the road. "You can leave me there if you want. I should be safe with so many people around. Colt wouldn't dare do anything in front of everyone."

He shook his handsome head. "I'm not leaving you alone. For as much as your safety means to me, I wouldn't leave you alone. And since we're together and I want to support you, I can't leave you alone in a time like this. I'll be your rock."

Her eyes welled with tears, and she silently chided herself for being weak. Just when she thought the crying was over, it wasn't.

45

Hannah came to visit with Lara, cookies in tow. They worked together in the kitchen as they brought in food and took care of removing the foil coverings and setting it out on the table. They replenished dishes as they emptied and as neighbors brought more food. She and Lara worked efficiently and calmly.

For his part, he was introduced as Kenna's boyfriend, Kenna's young man, Kenna's man over and over. He'd met so many people from this town and others, he wouldn't remember their names.

He looked across the small living room to Kenna. She was speaking with an older lady who nodded her head, then patted Kenna on the shoulder and stepped away. Kenna took a deep breath and caught his eye.

Her weary smile told him volumes about how she felt right now. He moved to close the distance between them, stepping around small groups of people talking and those carrying plates of food to a chair or sofa.

When he was close enough to touch her, he pulled her into his arms and held her close. Her arms wrapped around his waist. They stood quietly for a few moments before she pulled away.

She tilted her head, and he grinned. "How are you doing?"

She shrugged. "Good." She leaned closer and whispered. "It's just so draining."

He only nodded in response, because he didn't know. But he felt tired of this right now too, and he'd only met Howie on his deathbed. Navigating the well-wishers and barrage of questions coming at her about the time of the service, and how she was doing and, mostly, was she staying here to keep the business going? He tried not listening to that answer because he wasn't ready to hear the response if she said she was leaving.

That thought right there made his heart feel like a hot rock had fallen on it. It hurt. A lot.

He shook his head to remove those thoughts and kissed the top of her head. "Have you eaten, honey?"

"No. I was waiting for you."

"Let's go eat now while there seems to be a lull."

She chuckled. "This is a lull?"

"It's the first one all day. The house is only half full right now."

He turned her toward the dining room and his mom met them halfway. "How are you two doing?"

He waited for Kenna to speak and was surprised when she gave a quiet response. "I know everyone means well, but this is really just too much."

His mom pulled Kenna into her arms and hugged her close. "It is a lot and they mean well. Except those two busybodies over there who are gathering gossip."

Kenna turned in the direction his mom nodded. When she turned back to his mom, her eyes rounded and she genuinely smiled for the first time today. "They're the worst in town. I don't even know if Mom and Dad know them, other than the gossip twins."

His mom chuckled. "That's a perfect name for them."

Kenna glanced back to make sure no one was listening, then whispered conspiratorially with his mom. "I think I served them once."

They shared a chuckle, and his heart swelled. That was nice to see and hear.

His mom stepped back. "You two need to eat something. So, grab a plate and maybe go to another room where you can have a moment for yourselves."

"Is that appropriate?" Kenna asked.

His mom winked. "Your brothers both did it."

Nodding, Kenna stepped toward the plates. "Those shits."

He kissed his mom's cheek. "Thanks for everything today, Mom."

She wrapped her arms around him and squeezed him close. "I'm happy to help."

He filled his plate and Kenna motioned toward her childhood bedroom. He followed her down the hall, holding his breath. No one stopped them and he released a sigh of relief when they made it without interruption.

They sat on her bed, too small for them to sit side by side against the headboard. "You sit and rest your back against the wall. I'll sit down here and stare at your gorgeous face."

She scoffed, but willingly rested against the headboard. They ate peacefully in relative silence. She finished her dinner and set her plate on her nightstand. She folded her hands in her lap and watched him for a few moments.

"What?" he asked.

"Do you want kids one day?"

His eyes rounded, and he swallowed his food. "Yes. Do you?"

"I do. When I think of what I want for my life, and I've been thinking of almost nothing but lately, I want dark-haired, green-eyed babies with a man I love more than anything else in the world."

He stared at her, frozen, not entirely sure what she meant. "Okay."

"I love you, Spencer." She tucked her hair behind her ear. "While we haven't had a conventional relationship to this point, we've been through things many couples don't ever experience. Every time, you've stood by me unquestioningly. Every. Time. I hope I will be as strong and careful and loving if you ever have tough times because I want to be that for you."

He set his plate on the desk behind him and scooted closer to Kenna. He took her hands in his hands and swallowed to give his heart time to slow down, because right now, it felt like it would beat right out of his chest.

"I love you, Kenna." He stared at their joined hands. Their fingers intertwined together. Their coloring was different. He was more tanned than she was. His hands were rougher, but she never complained. His fingers were much larger than hers, but she always seemed to enjoy touching him. Holding hands with him. Being near him. "I want dark-haired, green-eyed babies with a woman who loves me with her whole heart."

"I love you with my whole heart," she breathed.

His throat tightened up and his heart, as impossible as it seemed, beat wildly. His breathing became quick breaths and his lungs felt like he couldn't take in enough air.

His voice cracked. "I love you with my whole heart."

She scooted closer to him, their legs folded in front of them, touching. Her hands framed his face, her thumbs smoothed over his lips, and he was lost in the most beautiful green eyes he'd ever seen. Jewels, they were like jewels.

She inhaled and slowly exhaled as her hands held his head in hers. "I want to stay here and run the business. I want to be in your life, and I so want you in mine. Despite the bad things that have happened since I've been home, the good things have far outweighed them. The good things are all you. Your strength. Your protectiveness. Your love. Your steady, constant presence. That's all you Spencer."

She leaned in and kissed him; he cradled the back of her head in his hand. He wanted to hold her here to him forever. Her lips molded to his, their softness wrapping his in her warmth.

She pulled slightly back and laid her forehead against his. Then she sat up and looked into his eyes. He grinned. He wanted to remember this moment—forever.

"Kenna Lawrence, will you be my wife and have my green-eyed, dark-haired babies?"

Her throat moved as she swallowed. Her lips formed the most beautiful smile, and her head nodded.

"I absolutely will. All of it. Be your wife. Have babies with you. Create a family and love you all my days."

46

They stood at the graveside as the minister said last rites before they lowered her father into the ground. Spencer's arm was firmly around her shoulders. His presence was always comforting.

The sun didn't shine today. For some reason, that seemed fitting. The cloudy day lent to the mood.

The minister finished his prayer, and she dutifully said, "Amen."

Spencer's parents had been present throughout, always there when they needed them. Never in the way or glomming for attention. Spencer was so much like his father, it was uncanny to watch them. Same facial expressions. Same laugh. Same gestures.

They hadn't told anyone they'd gotten engaged. It wasn't the right time and she sort of enjoyed having a happy secret. Spencer wanted them to get through the funeral, then go to Brookswood and buy a ring to make it official. They'd tell everyone after.

She turned and hugged her mom. Then Spencer's parents, then her brothers.

Spencer took her hand in his and led her to his truck. His parents walked with them. Her brothers took their mom by the arms and walked just ahead of them.

Spencer said, "Mom and Dad, will you be joining us for lunch?"

His mom responded, "Yes. We'll go there with you both."

He grinned but said nothing else. He helped Kenna into the backseat of his truck. His mom sat with her. He and his father in the front.

Her phone chimed a text, and she pulled it up and gasped. Wyatt turned quickly. "Let me see it."

She quietly handed her phone to him. Spencer's eyes glanced at her in the mirror. Spencer's phone chimed a text then, and he pulled it from his pocket and handed it to his dad.

She'd received another anonymous text from the mysterious only-nines number of her standing next to Spencer at the gravesite.

She leaned forward to see what he'd received, and Wyatt held up Spencer's phone and showed her. It was a picture of Kenna hugging Spencer's parents at the gravesite.

"I didn't see him there. I wasn't looking, but I think I would have noticed him."

Spencer's jaw was tight when he responded, "I was watching and didn't see him at all."

Wyatt tapped on the phones, seemingly to send the pictures off to Cyber or Tate then handed her phone back to her.

"You don't need to keep it?" she asked.

"No. We've got enough texts to hang him when we

confirm it's him. Or whoever it is. I forwarded these on, so they can keep them as evidence."

She nodded, dropped her phone into her shoulder bag, and decided not to look at it again today.

As Spencer pulled into the church parking lot, his phone rang.

"Hi, Tate."

"Hey, is this a good time?"

Spencer turned back to look at her, his brows raised. She nodded.

"Yeah, it's good."

"We have the IP address. It's at a business in town called Networking Solutions."

Her brows bunched together. She'd never heard of it. Spencer responded, "Okay."

Tate continued, "So, we've pulled up the information on Networking Solutions and found it only has two employees, both of them owners. Daniel Juergensen and Ami Pearson."

She gasped. Spencer turned in his seat and locked eyes with her. "Colt's fiancée?"

She nodded.

Spencer responded to Tate. "Ami Pearson is Colt Lowe's fiancée. We saw her in the store the other day."

"Well, son of a bitch. I'll get the sheriff out there to her business right away."

Spencer added. "She just sent us pictures at the gravesite of us. So, if she isn't at work, look for her car. Send Dad and me her car's description so we can watch for her here at the church."

"I'll send that over now. I'd like to let the sheriff handle this, Spence. It's not really something we've been asked to do, and the sheriff will have jurisdiction."

Spencer replied, "We understand."

"Okay. Out."

Spencer heaved out a deep breath and jumped out of the truck. Her door opened and he reached in to help her down. Her legs were shaking, her mouth was dry and she held on to him for dear life.

His arms were powerful around her as he hurried them into the church. Inside, he turned and looked out the window for a long time before his parents finally entered.

Wyatt softly said, "She isn't out there. Not in her vehicle, anyway."

"Okay. Thanks, Dad."

Spencer looked into her eyes. "Are you alright?"

"Yeah. It's a relief actually. I'm scared of Colt. I've never been scared of Ami."

"You won't have to be scared of her ever again."

She nodded and tried to smile, but she felt frozen in the information overload. They began descending the steps to the basement, and she murmured, "It makes sense."

"What does, honey?"

"The direction of that first picture of me all beaten up. It came from the law office. Jessie, the receptionist there. I don't know her married last name. She and Ami were friends throughout school and when I picked up papers to serve on Craig and Kent, Jessie made sure to tell me Colt was engaged to Ami. I'll bet she took that picture and sent it to Ami."

"That makes her an accomplice to stalking."

At the bottom of the steps, she heaved out a big breath and located the table where her mom and brothers sat.

The four of them hurried over to the table and Kenna sat with a plop before her wobbly knees gave out.

Her mom gasped slightly. "Kenna, are you alright? You're pale as a ghost."

"Yes. I'm fine. Just some bad news. It'll be fine, Mama."

Sean looked at her from across the table, his brows hidden behind his bangs. She merely shook her head to stave off questioning.

A commotion sounded at the top of the stairs and soon the sheriff and Officer Gordon ran down the stairs and into the room.

Sheriff hollered, "Everyone, please stay in your seats for a moment."

Officer Gordon ran past and into the kitchen. A clatter of pans hitting the floor and a couple women yelling filtered out to the room and Spencer and Wyatt both jumped up to see what was going on. She watched as the sheriff said something, then nodded when he recognized Spencer.

Yvette reached over and took her hand and she moved over into Spencer's seat to sit next to her future mother-in-law. Though Yvette didn't know that yet.

Screaming filled the air and then the words, "I want that bitch out of here."

She swallowed, and her breathing came in spurts. Yvette squeezed her hand tighter, and she felt an equal amount of fear and hope.

Finally, Officer Gordon came into the room from the kitchen with Ami Pearson in handcuffs.

"Oh my God!" Kenna exclaimed.

Yvette leaned close. "Is that her?"

"Yes."

Ami's eyes sought hers, and when they finally locked on each other, Ami snarled. "Get. Out. Of. Town."

She swallowed a rock that had formed in her throat and tears streamed down her face. It was all just too much.

Spencer rushed over to them and pulled her to her feet, then wrapped his arms around her. "It's okay, sweetheart. She won't bother you again."

"I've never seen such hate," she said into his chest.

"People do weird things to others, honey. After they question her, we'll see what her intentions were. It seems like she was simply trying to scare you away."

Her brother Sean came close. "Kenna, do you know what that was all about?"

She nodded. "She's engaged to Colt Lowe."

"And?"

Spencer kept her close, but spoke to Sean. "She's been stalking Kenna since she's been home. It's been stressful."

"Kenna, why didn't you say something?"

She took a deep breath before responding. "With Daddy so sick at first and then passing, I just didn't want anyone else to worry." She looked into Spencer's handsome face. "Spencer's been taking care of me. Protecting me. Rescuing me."

47

Spencer stared at Kenna's finger. The ring they'd picked out gleamed brightly in the sun. He'd never spent so much on such a little thing, but he was so proud to see it on her finger right now.

He drove them toward the HOG, where everyone would be eating dinner now. It was his parents' last day in town, and he and Kenna had begged off for a bit of time today. He told them they had some things to wrap up at Kenna's cousin's house. A little white lie he'd apologize for later.

"It's so beautiful, Spencer."

He looked into her eyes, and his smile grew. "It is. It still doesn't rival you, though."

She laughed. "You always make me feel special."

He lifted her left hand and kissed her fingers. "When are we getting married, Kenna?"

She heaved out a deep breath. "I don't know. Of course, I want my brothers here. I don't know when they can get back. What about your parents and Dani? When will they be able to come back here for a wedding?"

He laughed. "My parents will be here whenever we tell them the date is. Dani, if I give her enough notice, she'll make it. So that brings us back to your brothers."

"Yeah. Maybe we can ask them when we tell them we're getting married."

He chuckled. "That sounds like a plan."

She grinned, and his mind whirled. Without a moment in between, he blurted out. "I want to get married right away. Maybe Mom and Dad can stay a few more days and we'll get married here. At the HOG. They can be here. Your brothers are still here. They can be here too."

She laughed; her face a sight to behold for certain. His mind reeled with all the things. He'd dreamed of being a father in the past, but after Aidyn and Elena had their baby, he began thinking of it more. He was thirty-one; it was time.

"How many kids do you want? It's something we should talk about."

She turned toward him in her seat. "Two, I think."

He squeezed her hand, then kissed her fingers. "Yeah. Two sounds perfect."

Kenna chuckled. "It's a great number."

He pulled into the HOG garage and shut the truck off. He jumped from the truck and hustled around to help Kenna down. When he opened the door, he smiled at her.

He kissed her lips. "So you really want to be here? Stay here I mean?"

Her arms wrapped around his shoulders, and he pulled her off her seat. Her legs immediately wrapped around his waist. "I don't want to be anywhere you aren't. That's the honest truth, Spencer."

His heart felt light and he couldn't wait to tell his parents. He let her body slide down his until her feet touched the ground. Taking her hand in his, he started them toward the door then stopped. "Let's go tell them we're getting married."

She smiled her beautiful smile. He'd watch her smile forever now, and that was a great feeling. "Okay."

He kissed her again, his heart happy. It was difficult to get his breathing under control and he wanted to shout. Literally, shout right now.

He opened the door to the HOG for her and walked in behind her. Their friends and family were eating and his mom jumped up to get plates for them.

"Hi, you two. Come on in and eat. We just started since we weren't sure when you'd be home."

"Thanks, Mom." He led Kenna to the table and they sat. His mom set their plates in front of them and sat next to his dad.

He didn't begin eating right away, but glanced down and stared into Kenna's eyes for a few beats. She smiled and nodded, then he said, "We have an announcement."

The room quieted, and he held up Kenna's left hand. "She said yes!"

Their friends cheered, and his mom jumped up from her seat and hugged Kenna. "Welcome to the family." Then she hugged him. "Congratulations, honey."

His dad shook his hand, then pulled him in for a hug. "Congratulations, son."

"Thanks, Dad."

Their friends gathered around and offered hugs and handshakes. He was elated. She was radiant. It was a moment he'd remember forever.

He inhaled a deep breath, then let it out slowly before leaving the bedroom in his tuxedo. Kenna and the women, including his mom, had had hair appointments that morning, then came back, and were getting ready in one of the spare bedrooms. He could hear the laughter as he passed, and he grinned.

"Hey, are you ready?" Henry asked from across the room.

"I— Henry, about you—?"

Henry scoffed. "I don't have to do anything but be there."

Tate exited his bedroom, the smile on his face broad. "Hey, how's the groom?"

Spencer laughed. "I'm fine. You look like a football player who just won the MVP award."

Tate shrugged. "I did. But I can't say anything just yet."

Spencer glanced at Henry and shrugged. Tate turned to Henry and said, "Tomorrow there's a crack negotiator coming in from the Department of Defense. Casper is sending her in to negotiate the last deal with the BRR.

Craig hasn't agreed to sit down and talk yet, but Gerard and Jasiah will get Craig on board, if we make some concessions. Those concessions are that power is run up the mountain before he'll sign anything. Casper and the town will work on an agreement with the negotiator. Her name is Everleigh Hayes. Casper has asked for protection for her since Kenna had issues when she first met Craig. I've offered your services, Henry."

"Thanks?" Henry rotated his shoulders. "Though between us, I hope Craig tries to pull something just so I can let go on him for all the shit he's done."

Spencer chuckled. "If you get that chance, give him an extra punch or two from Kenna and me."

"Happily."

Tate grinned. "And, Spencer, the sheriff called. It appears Ami acted on her own accord. Colt didn't tell her Kenna was in town. She took that as a lie of omission and they argued. He started his anger management classes again and she became unhinged, Colt's words, not mine. She accused him of going to classes for Kenna and not her. Apparently, they've had issues in the past. Anyway, it apparently became too much for Ami and she snapped. I'm not sure what the future holds for those two, either together or apart. They both have legal issues to contend with now."

Spencer shook Tate's hand. "Thanks for the update. It'll make Kenna feel better knowing what's going on. And, I admit, it's been bothering me too."

His dad opened his bedroom door and stared at them. "I haven't worn a tux in a while. I feel stiff as a board."

"You look great, Dad. I'm trying to remember the last time I saw you in a tux."

"I think it was your cousin's wedding."

Spencer's eyes widened. "It's been a while."

His dad grinned. "You look great, Spencer."

His dad glanced at Henry, his best man, in his tux. Then he nodded to Tate. "You guys both look great, too. I don't want to leave anyone out."

They laughed, and Spencer fidgeted with his cuff links. He wanted to get the ceremony part over.

His dad chucked him on the shoulder. "They'll be out soon. Your mom texted me to make sure we were ready just before I left the bedroom. Let's head outside."

He followed his friends, his dad at his side. "I'm proud of you, Spencer."

He glanced at his dad and grinned. "Thanks, Dad. I'm so glad you and mom are here."

His dad scoffed. "As if your mom would ever miss it. Dani sent her love and said she'll call you later. She couldn't get away on such short notice."

He chuckled. "She called me last night and this morning. I know she feels bad. It's understandable. Hopefully, I'll take Kenna out to see Dani in a couple of weeks."

They stepped outside, and he looked around at the transformation that had happened so quickly. They'd set up an arbor across the lawn and arranged white wooden folding chairs with an aisle between them. Kenna's brothers were helping to set up additional chairs with Myles and Maya. He waved to them and they smiled and waved back.

A man with a guitar was strumming a soft tune, his amplifier just loud enough to be heard. A man came up alongside him. "It's time, Spencer."

He turned to see the minister's smiling face. He grinned at the older man and shook his hand. "I'm ready, Pastor."

The pastor called out. "Please take your seats. We're about to begin."

He glanced at Henry and they walked to the front of the white chairs near the arbor strewn with flowers.

The guests, which were mostly his teammates, Kenna's mom and brothers, and a few family friends here in town.

His mom appeared near the end of the aisle, his dad held his arm out to her, and they walked toward him. His dad shook his hand and leaned in for a hug. "I love you, Spencer."

"I love you too, Dad."

His mom hugged him to her. Her arms squeezed him tightly, and he heard her sniff quietly. He chuckled. "I love you, Mom."

His mom's watery eyes looked into his. "I love you too, honey."

His dad grinned and helped his mom to their seats in the front row before she started crying in earnest.

Sean and Jon escorted their mom down the aisle next. He smiled at his new mother-in-law, who'd had a whirlwind week. She'd buried a husband and now was watching her only daughter get married. He shook Sean and Jon's hands, and hugged Niya close. "Thank you for making such an incredible woman."

"Thank you for seeing her incredibleness and keeping her safe and loved."

"It's my pleasure, Niya. Always."

Her sons led her to her seat on the other side of the aisle.

Lara and Henry walked down the aisle next. Henry was his best man and Lara, Kenna's matron of honor. Tate winked at his wife as she passed by and she reached out and touched his shoulder. Henry, the gentleman always, walked Lara to her position, then came to stand next to him, shaking his hand first.

The music changed, and everyone stood. He saw her, her dark hair gleaming in the sunlight, her smile rivaling the sun. She wore a white dress Shianne had found for her. Not an official wedding dress, but it was perfect for her. The tea length gown, at least that's what Kenna had told him it was, fit her perfectly. The skirt billowed out slightly which made her look tinier than she was. She was princess perfect.

She'd opted to walk down the aisle alone. She'd told her family, in her mind, her father was walking with her and no one could take his place. Her mom cried when she'd announced this and said it was perfect. She even walked to one side of the aisle, making room for Howie's presence.

When she stopped before him, he smiled and stared at her. He wanted to commit this moment to memory, just like the other moments they'd had together. "You're stunning, Kenna."

She beamed. Literally beamed. "You're incredibly handsome, Spencer."

He winked, held his arm out to her and they took the final two steps toward the minister together.

As the minister opened his Bible, Spencer leaned down and whispered, "I can't wait to start on the children we talked about. Thank you for that."

ALSO BY PJ FIALA

You can find all of my books at https://pjfiala.com/books

Romantic Suspense

Rolling Thunder Series

Moving to Love, Book 1

Moving to Hope, Book 2

Moving to Forever, Book 3

Moving to Desire, Book 4

Moving to You, Book 5

Moving On, Book 6

Rolling Thunder Boxset 1, Books 1-3

Rolling Thunder Boxset 2, Books 4-6

Military Romantic Suspense

Second Chances Series

Designing Samantha's Love, Book 1

Securing Kiera's Love, Book 2

Bluegrass Security Series

Heart Thief, Book One

Finish Line, Book Two

Lethal Love, Book Three

Wrenched Fate, Book Four

Lynyrd Station Protectors - Security

Finding His Fire Book One

Finding His Mark Book Two

Finding His Jewel Book Three

Finding His Match Book Four

Big 3 Security Boxset, Books 1-3

Lynyrd Station Protectors - Special Ops

Defending Keirnan, LSP Special Ops Book One

Defending Sophie, LSP Special Ops Book Two

Defending Roxanne, LSP Special Ops Book Three

Defending Yvette, LSP Special Ops BookFour

Defending Bridget, LSP Special Ops Book Five

Defending Isabella, LSP Special Ops Book Six

LSP Special Ops Box Set One (Books 1-3)

LSP Special Ops Box Set Two (Books 4-6)

Lynyrd Station Protectors - Trafficking

RAPTOR Rising - Prequel

Saving Shelby, LSP Trafficking Book One

Holding Hadleigh, LSP Trafficking Book Two

Craving Charlesia, LSP Trafficking Book Three

Promising Piper, LSP Trafficking Book Four

Missing Mia, LSP Trafficking Book Five

Believing Becca, LSP Trafficking Book Six

Keeping Kori, LSP Trafficking Book Seven

Healing Hope, LSP Trafficking Book Eight

Engaging Emersyn, LSP Trafficking Book Nine

LSP Trafficking Box Set 1

LSP Trafficking Box Set 2

LSP Trafficking Box Set 3

GHOST Legacy (Next generation)

Finding Lara, Book One

Saving Elena, Book Two

Rescuing Kenna, Book Three

Protecting Everleigh, Book Four

Guarding Adelaide, Book Five

Shielding Maya, Book Six

MEET PJ

Writing has been a desire my whole life. Once I found the courage to write, life changed for me in the most profound way. Bringing stories to readers that I'd enjoy reading and creating characters that are flawed, but lovable is such a joy.

When not writing, I'm with my family doing something fun. My husband, Gene, and I are bikers and enjoy riding to new locations, meeting new people and generally enjoying this fabulous country we live in.

I come from a family of veterans. My grandfather, father, brother, two sons, and one daughter-in-law are all veterans. Needless to say, I am proud to be an American and proud of the service my amazing family has given.

My online home is https://www.pjfiala.com.
You can connect with me on
Facebook: https://www.facebook.com/PJFialaAuthor
Instagram: https://www.Instagram.com/PJFiala.
YouTube: https://youtube.com/@PJFiala
TikTok: https://www.tiktok.com/@pjfiala?lang=en
If you prefer to email, go ahead, I'll respond - pjfiala@
pjfiala.com.